A Life Well Lived

Beverly Dewhirst

Author's Page

Beverly Dewhirst is a proud British citizen with only a trace of a Canadian accent. She relocated to the land of her heart and heritage on July 30 2011 and it suits, as she always knew it would. It suits very well thank-you.

G.B.B.

Dedicated

With love

to

Paul Dewhirst

And

Margery Dennett

My parents.

Acknowledgements

Ta Very Much

To

Helen Davies, who dragged me kicking and screaming from my comfort zone,

Sylvia Kemp, for her 'delightful' workshops,

And

Fellow scribblers of Congleton U3A writing groups.

For

Encouragement and feedback, a writer's sustenance.

Chapter One

They said I'd be safer and happier but until then I didn't know I wasn't safe and happy. All my meals would be served in delightful surroundings with compatible company. Bloody hell, I already have my own homey, comfortable kitchen and you never know when someone unexpected might pop in to share my latest concoction; declaring it to border just short of gourmet cuisine. And furthermore, my idea of compatible company is someone with a functioning brain, who knows how to argue a point just short of murder then ask if I want them to wash or dry. Another so called benefit brought to my attention was a menu card selection, outlining the coming week's food choices. Personally I prefer to pull something out of the freezer, analyse the contents, choosing the one with the least likely risk of food poisoning and zap it in the microwave or bung it in the oven: all to be accomplished within thirty minutes before I think I'm starving to death. That's my idea of menu planning whether I have company or not and I have every intention of continuing along those lines. The days of catering to individual tastes are finally a thing of the past. Somehow I fell into that trap when the children were young but time has moved on and I'm moving right along with it.

On the latest familial duty call a much perused brochure was thrust into my hands. It dealt with further information on my dutiful children's final attempt to lure me into their deviously conceived lair. An outstanding activity program for residents of all levels, it proclaimed. All levels of what I inwardly question, as I grasp the once glossy, brochure describing said marvellous program. Smiles all around as the group continue to mouth with less than believable enthusiasm their extreme good fortune to have discovered such an establishment. Another not so subtle attempt to reassure me even someone with my strange interests would find something acceptable here. A quick glance informs me of what's on offer at the moment. Crafts, artificial flower arranging, in mini size only, Bingo, Shuffle-Board and the Bean Bag Toss from a sitting position. If the mornings weren't your best time the program would be offered again in the afternoon and you'd have the chance to join in with just with one minor concession. To accommodate the more athletic and competitive residents wishing to participate in the Bean Bag Toss, the game would be played from an upright stance. A happy hour commences at two o'clock on Fridays and offers absolutely gratis, a wee dram of whisky or for the more genteel a small glass of sherry. Yes I think to myself, and both diluted with pure tap water just out of sight of the anxiously waiting elderly ravers. Imagine the excitement, all this with the added challenge of participating in the advanced bean bag toss for those specialists of multitasking from bygone days.

Quoting from the brochure I read aloud, 'we like to think of ourselves as one big family so dinner is served promptly at four o'clock. From past experience we have determined that if we serve at a later time, some of our more elderly residents will nod off, to the extent of laying their heads on the table. Needless to say because of this we do insist on punctuality'

Yes, yes I thought, understandably a strange head resting near one's pudding could prove to have a somewhat disturbing effect on those who were looking forward to their blancmange.

Where did I go wrong? What makes them think I would even consider this drivel? I guess when I retired four years ago they became concerned that at some point in the near future I might ask to live with one of them. The likelihood of that happening is the same as me becoming queen.

Shortly after my retirement I was faced with the shocking realization I was not in a good position financially. Because of misguided generosity I had allowed myself to fall into a very vulnerable and precarious state. Now at a time when I no longer had the opportunity to rebuild my savings I would definitely have to make do on a low and fixed budget. The truth of it was I had squandered my retirement funds on my ungrateful brood when they said they 'needed' some help. Now I had to face the fact that my reduced income would not allow for the little extras we all look forward to in later life. It appears I was in the sad and seemingly hopeless position of 'not having a pot to pee in' so to speak, and it shook me to the core. Shedding more than a few tears of self-pity I had to face the fact I had brought it upon myself. Thankfully, acknowledging where to lay the blame also gave me the insight of where to look for the solution and now, I'm happy to say I've found it, or think I've found it. My answer to the problem is really quite straightforward. Having accepted that the sands of life will continue to run whether I enter the race or not, I've made the decision to lace up my trainers and see if I can not only compete but take the lead as well.

The first decision I make is that I'm going to have a holiday, my kind of holiday. I want to relish my golden years in a golden way, albeit minus the gold. Bugger it, what I want is adventure, the kind I used to have and the kind I mean to have again and I propose to begin now, this very minute.

Surveying myself in the looking glass I'm reminded of Alice, growing larger and smaller at the whim of a nibble of cake or a sip from a bottle. Unfortunately I may have consumed too many sips and nibbles and am now a greatly enlarged version of that sylph like adventurous blonde. I choose to think of myself as having a slightly Rubenesque figure while grudgingly acknowledge the fact I shall never again be the femme fatale I never was in the first place. Nevertheless, I'm not willing to give up at the first hurdle so my personal assessment of redeeming features continues. How bloody depressing, nary a one jumps out at me. This means some serious thought is necessary.

Inspecting my wardrobe used to inspire me so that's where I'll start. After two hours of emptying the closet, disgorging drawers, and generally turning my bedroom into a skip, I can tell right now this will not be one of my better days. Heaven help the poor unsuspecting soul that darkens my doorway for any reason other than to tell me I've won that lottery. Unfortunately there's little chance of that for I haven't bought a ticket these past five years. Maybe a glass of something will boost my mood and offer some spiritual inspiration. They don't refer to alcohol as spirits for nothing you know.

Believe it or not a generous libation has generated a thought. I used to have a lot of those, thoughts I mean. Well alright, maybe a few generous libations too but who's business is it but mine? Forgive me I regress, another dare I say it, shortcoming of those of my generation. But the thing is, up until now those thoughts have conspired against me joining the ever flowing sands of time to depart from my mind as quickly as they arrived. But with my new outlook I have conceived an exciting idea that has caused my mind to focus, and it may just work. It is so simple as to be brilliant and the worst that can happen is, well... maybe the worst that can happen. Don't give a fancy damn, I'm on my way.

First to be salvaged during the wardrobe excavation is a slightly shabby, dark grey, trouser suit. It doesn't matter that the waistband no longer sits at my waist, it adds a bit more leg length if ones frontal excess is allowed to remain unrestricted, to find it's own space somewhere above the lowered waistband of the trousers. A permanently buttoned jacket will hide the resulting obscenity to fashion. Oh, I always loved this soft grey, ruffle fronted blouse. It will be perfect if I just move the buttons over a bit. No sense further inflaming passions by a gaping maw showing the formerly awesome but now somewhat less elevated bosom. Must look into one of those wired push up bras they advertise. It will cut into the budget a bit but perky never did any harm. Also a pair of those underpants that grab and hoist you somewhere you've not been in thirty years could be worth the extra dosh too. Can't afford two pair so I'll wear everyday bargain brands underneath to change every day and the quality stuff won't need to be washed as often. Inspecting my old black leather boots I'm confident the scuff marks can be hidden with a coat or two of polish so overall it's an encouraging beginning and I feel a certain amount of optimism. Last to be unearthed is a wonderful black cape that had been delegated to the back of the wardrobe and had since fallen from its hanger and lain in a heap for who knows how long.

Can't even remember why I bought it but now, just for fun, I throw it over my shoulders and immediately feel transformed. Dated yes, but with just a touch of class from days gone by. All that's missing is a black slouch hat, one I can dip to one side and peer from under. Bloody hell, where is it? It's got to be here somewhere. I remember buying it for a fancy dress party, yes, yes, and that's when I bought the cape too. Eureka, here it is, I still have it!

Suddenly the room has become uncomfortably warm and my heart begins to pound, threatening to jump into my throat. Quickly opening the window I stand before it and force myself to take deep, slow breaths, in and out, in and out. While the cool reviving air bathes my flushed face I struggle for inner control but, as I glance down at my hands resting on the window sill, I'm shocked to see they've taken on a life of their own; shaking as if keeping time to an inner rhythm. A heightened feeling of giddiness washes over me and I'm aware my pulse is racing too. Damn it anyway, just as I've found a reason to live is it all going to be snatched away from me in an instant? Am I about to snuff it?

No I am not! Offering sincere thanks to God amid imaginary background strains of the Hallelujah chorus, I recognize that all but forgotten wonderful high called excitement and anticipation coursing through my veins, dragging me back to life. My life, a real life filled with endless zest to explore the wonders of each new day. Serendipity, precious gift that it is, now freely offered and within my grasp. Easily accepted in exchange for the lifeless existence my supposed dearest ones would have me believe is in my best interest.

With renewed confidence my demise is not imminent I go back to the task at hand. Next I unearth an old travel case. Looking it over I have to admit, even in it's better days it would never have fooled anyone as having been quality luggage. But as so often happens, a supposedly useless article offers its own surprise gift. Long forgotten but neatly tucked away in one of the zippered pockets is a pair of trousers and two more tops, admittedly a bit snug, but they'll do for now.

Now finally at day's end, it seems the next logical step is a trip to the charity shops is what is called for. To-morrow I'll venture forth with high hopes of finding something that speaks of class, albeit financed from a pauper's purse. This has been a good day, my adventure's beginning, even though I'm damn near skint. I'm excited and optimistic, and for the first time in a long while I'm looking forward to what a new day brings. An added bonus is I'm just plain tired so think I'll sleep well to-night.

Chapter Two

Day two of my new undertaking has me up bright and early. I plan to catch the nine-thirty bus to that footballer's town about an hour and a half away. The female population, 'wags' as they're known, spend a small fortune on clothing and while I may be limited by their size zero dresses, there's bound to be some cast off donated by their chubby overindulged Mums that will suit me.

I can't believe my good fortune, first shop I enter I spot a great looking case for five pounds. Inspecting the inside I'm aware of a peculiar odour, so maybe that's the reason for the low price tag on such a quality piece. It's a lovely rich burgundy colour and I want it so much I convince myself I'll find a way to get rid of the offensive smell. The next two shops yield nothing of use to me but just as I'm ready to call it a day, I hear a fellow scrounger say to the woman standing next to her, that she always saves the best till last. This comment piques my curiosity and I hover close, continuing to browse, feigning interest in a scarf, while in fact I was only waiting for her to leave the building. As she makes her exit I trail behind and furtively shadow her up the high street till she turns down a narrow alley, making towards the smallest shop imaginable. Forging ahead I reach her just in time to follow upon her heels through the front door.

Immediately an unfamiliar scent assails my nostrils but so completely taken in with with the interior of the room, which is quite outlandish compared to other charity shops, I quickly forget the odour. A youngish looking middle aged woman standing behind a small, cluttered counter smiled at both of us and said, 'feel free to browse, I'm just stepping out back for a smoke.'

Hmm, I thought, a bit unusual to give total strangers free reign to help themselves if they chose to do so. Nevertheless, the woman who had led me to this so called 'best for last' saw nothing odd in this behaviour so I joined her and went about rifling through the racks. Finally my bargain hunter cohort announced with a sigh she could find nothing new since her last visit and wishing me a hearty good luck and good bye, she departed. The tinny tinkle of the overhead bell as the door opened and closed reminded me I was alone so I set about in earnest to discover any bargains that suited my needs. I find so many things I like. My problem is being reasonable and only purchasing what would benefit my upcoming plans. The shop owner reappears and asks how I'm doing. Holding up my treasures for her to see I say, ' I like so many things it's difficult to choose.'

To my amazement her reply is, 'good take them all, pay what you can afford and be sure to visit again.'

I was stunned and could only continue to stare at her. She smiled ever so kindly and gave a barely audible soft laugh which served to bring me back to myself. Quickly accepting that ever since I'd entered the premises the atmosphere had been slightly bizarre, I fumbled and rifled through my handbag eventually finding a total of just over six pounds in coins. Slightly ashamed to offer such a pittance I presented all in my open palm, beginning to explain I thought the amount I had to spend was insulting for the amount of goods lying on the counter.

'No, no, it's fine,' she said, cutting me off in mid-sentence. I tipped the coins into her hand and even without counting them she tossed them under the counter and began to fold the garments. I think she noticed the odour coming from my case and thoughtfully put my purchases in carrier bags before storing them inside it. I thanked her for her generosity and promised to return. As I opened the door to leave the shop she called out to me saying the odour from my case would dissipate if I left it outdoors for a night or two with rosemary sprigs inside all the pockets. Thanking her again for her help I closed the tiny shop door and happily made my way to the bus stop.

On the trip home, reflecting on my morning's adventure, I was once again caught up in the excitement of it all. As if in collusion and to fuel the sensation the bus jostled my parcels more than usual, so as I had to grasp them tightly which served to remind me of the reason I had bought them in the first place. In this heightened state of mind the next train of thought was inevitable. I became firmly convinced it was a premonition of much greater things to come, so much so that anybody looking at me would have wondered why a solitary woman was smiling for no apparent reason.

I could hardly wait to get inside the house and unpack my bargains. The one extravagance is a very posh black lace nightie. Definitely too sheer for someone my age unless I wanted to wear knickers and a vest underneath, or better still, a long chemise. Daft I know but I had to have it, if only to reassure myself that I'd once turned a few heads in my time. To make amends for succumbing to vanity and the resulting useless nightie, there is a very practical black, long sleeve pullover with a generous cowl collar. A style guaranteed to hide the ravages of turkey neck syndrome when the soft cashmere is arranged in flowing folds. Light blue denim jeans with an elasticised waistband, a recently discovered necessity for comfort, and a western type plaid shirt. The shirt is surprisingly feminine considering the style. With its unobtrusive trim of lace at collar and cuffs, it speaks of a designer who loved fabric and gave much thought to the smallest detail. Nice pair of well fitting, almost new black leather gloves, and three sheer scarves that had seen better days. The scarves were not intended for warmth but as flashy accessories to be draped over the shoulders. They had a few snags here and there but I was sure I could transform them into something wearable. At the bottom of the last bag lay a tiny hand stitched cotton pouch. Pulling the draw string open I saw what appeared to be a small amount of tobacco.

Closing it to prevent the contents from spilling I realized it must have been on the counter when my clothes were being folded so made a mental note to return it when I visit the shop again, which I'll surely do. The owner was such an openly friendly woman, reminding me of the time of the hippies. Not that I was one, my flower children were produced within a happy marriage, knowing the identity of both parents. Oh, isn't that a hoot? Best not to dwell on the past though, guaranteed to bring on a filthy mood. I've got some fantastic buys and that's how I'm going to remember the day.

All that's left now is to organize my itinerary. The first part of my new life, because that's how I think of it and what it's going to become is this. I'll use my bus pass for free transportation to English towns. Upon arrival at hotels or guest houses with my business card in hand, must get those printed, I'll ask to speak to the manager and with that meeting will come the commitment. If all goes as planned I'll be in charge of my own life once again and on my way to another wonderful adventure. The kind I haven't had in, oh who knows how long? My overall plan might seem a bit daft to some but even if it fails I will have at the very least brightened up my life and reassured myself I'm not ready for the knacker's yard yet.

Chapter Three

Next morning after a general tidy up around the house I return to my bedroom and stand in front of the full length mirror in preparation to rehearsing my spiel. Taking a moment to adjust my posture and fix my features in what I feel is a professional and business like demeanour, I begin to practice what I'd composed last night. Pretending I'm in the lobby and at the front desk of a hotel, business card in hand and in full sight, I'll request the presence of whoever is in charge saying, 'Good afternoon, may I speak to your manager?' Depending upon the response, I begin my patter or wait for the appropriate personnel to arrive. This is when I present my business card and while the manager is scanning it I introduce myself formally.

'As a senior representative for a Canadian based company my task is to search out and sanction certain types of lodgings. The company's only prerequisite for their recommendation is a willingness to cater to the active and affluent elderly arriving from overseas. The prime reason for their visit to Britain is a long held wish to experience living in a typical English town. The stay is generally four days and all our clientele pay cash. They still don't approve of paying with plastic money, if you know what I mean. My job is to visit your premises and determine whether it and your staff would be conducive to a pleasant stay for our patrons. Naturally, it would not be appropriate to secure accommodation for them in any establishment catering to stag and hen parties or such. We look for more up market businesses at competitive prices.'

At this point I'll pause a moment and politely inquire if they would be interested in securing such an endorsement. If I receive a positive reply I'll reassure them of their wise decision and casually mention that it's extremely good advertising at an incredibly meagre rate. Not giving time for this announcement to register, thereby stifling any unnerving interruptions, I casually add their one and only outlay is to provide me with basic room and board while I complete my assessment of their operation. It is now I must be prepared for what could possibly be a deal breaker. The question of when I would like to book to make my assessment is yet to be faced. This is undoubtedly my greatest hurdle. Yet I must let them proceed with their queries so I stand fully engaged and at their beck and call. As the conversation continues I'll ever so slightly raise my chin a bit higher with a slight look of indignation but, upon absorbing the nature of their concerns I bend forward so as to hang on to their every word, all the while gently modifying my body posture. When they have concluded speaking and await my response, I deliver the final coupe de grace, as I tell them of the impossibility of completing an honest appraisal if undertaken with prior notice.

'No, no, definitely not allowed. You must understand pre booking would seriously compromise my report which must be totally unbiased, not only for the benefit of the company I represent but for your fine establishment also. I must submit my findings on what I find when you were not expecting a check, just an ordinary day so to speak.'

Then to soften the blow I engage my most comforting voice to reassure them this is not difficult and I ever so gently reiterate. 'I can honestly say staff, service and courtesy rate as high as surroundings so please don't think you have to do anything out of the ordinary, just be yourself and my work can be completed and submitted within two days, three at most. Upon approval of the submitted report you'll receive correspondence from the company and if agreeable to both, be offered fully non refundable deposits at that time.'

Again I quickly follow this with a mention that due to my experience, I foresee a very promising outlook of the suitability of their establishment therefore, would be most willing to settle immediately and get started on my appraisal.

Well I thought, needs a little fine tuning but don't want to sound too rehearsed. Sincerity and my unchanged Canadian accent will be my most believable selling point. Hot damn, I hadn't been this energized since, hmm, oh well it's been a long time but he really was lovely.

Devoting the rest of the day to washing, brushing, polishing, and doing a few alterations has paid off handsomely. The cape and slouch hat have come up a treat. I decided to snip off a ratty bit from the end of one scarf and wound the tattered piece around the crown of the hat. Securing it with a faux antique brooch it looks positively smashing and then I remember a beautiful, silky, grey, heron feather I'd saved. Damn, where was it? I couldn't possibly have thrown it away. I loved it and remember the spring day I found it while walking around Astbury Mere. Books from shelves tumbled down but no, I wouldn't have pressed it. That would have spoiled the silken, fragile, fronds. I must have stood it upright in a seldom used vase or something. I know, I know, it's in the back bedroom with some past loved, dried and dusty flowers. Brilliant, you're absolutely brilliant, I announced to no one in particular. A genius in disguise I tell myself, as I open the door to see the treasured old pint glass displaying the perfect embellishment to my outdated chapeau.

It's early evening and feeling more than a little smug, I sip a glass of wine while I ponder my first destination and make notes of jobs to do in the upcoming days. To-morrow I'll iron whatever needs it and visit the bank to withdraw a few precious pounds for travel expenses. I've decided to sacrifice the purchase of posh new undergarments in exchange for having an emergency fund. Heaven forbid if I should have to fork out cash for a bed but I really am past camping out or sitting up all night in a rail station.

Three more sleeps to H – Day, my acronym for Holiday, or God forbid, Hell Day.

This morning was very busy. A trip to the bank first thing then a little shopping before ordering business cards and finally the walk home. I spend the rest of the afternoon secreting pound notes in zippered pockets of my handbag and a cleverly hidden inner pocket of my cape. An outer cape pocket gives easy access to an assortment of coins for incidentals and my bus pass, thereby avoiding fumbling in my handbag at the last minute. My once not so sweet smelling travel case has completely lost its offensive odour and I pack most of my belongings inside. Come day's end I'm tired but reflect it's a good kind of tired. The planning has lifted my spirits and given me something to look forward to and I'm energized at the thought of what the next few days hold in store. I'm living the good life again and am not only filled with excitement at my anticipated adventure, but experience an almost overwhelming feeling of gratitude. I feel so humble to think I must have done something right in my lifetime to be given a second chance at such happiness. I don't question or doubt my feelings but hold them close and cherish them. I never want to forget this feeling of gratitude.

A new day and I'm up early and off to town with a rough copy of an appraisal form. I'm headed for the library to use their computer and printer. Library personnel are so helpful and thanks to them the finished form is very official looking. My plan is when I'm sure of being observed by my holiday hosts, I want to appear to be rating and recording my observations. Sometimes I surprise myself, I didn't know I had it in me to be quite so devious. After a much needed cup of coffee at the bus station's newly renovated café, I stop by the local shop to pick up my business cards. I'm impressed by the work, plain yet business like with the logo of a little grey mouse in the bottom left hand corner. Fanciful of me I know but I couldn't resist seeing my surname Graymouse represented without anyone being the wiser. My pseudonym is similar but pronounced differently and I seriously doubt anyone will ever take time to connect the two. My last errand is to purchase a few things for a packed lunch while travelling. I'm taking a flask of coffee, biscuits and sandwiches to save money on the first day's travel. Riding the bus home I try to think of what else remains to be done. Realistically, this first trip will certainly not be one of relaxation and enjoyed as a typical tourist. There will be more than a fair amount of work and fine tuning involved if it is to be the successful prototype for future adventures.

It's evening and once again I'm completely tuckered out from my day's chores. I more than welcome the retreat to my quiet garden. It's peaceful here, and splayed out in a garden chair with feet up on a discarded flower pot, I let my mind wander at will. Of course everything hinges on selling my slightly fraudulent scheme, I know that only too well. Success will be rewarded by some unknowing publican happily offering me tasty meals and a comfy bed, all compliments of the house. Failure, well I refuse to even contemplate failure. However should it occur, I suspect there will be ample time to plan another adventure while availing myself of free accommodation at the local nick. Oh perish the thought! And there would be the unwanted publicity too. My startled face appearing on the front page of the papers. I can see it now, 'British pensioner defrauds our neighbourhood business. The town council are asking to have the death penalty reinstated.' Stop, stop I chastise myself, you're making something out of nothing and looking for trouble where there is none. Get a grip! So much for letting the mind wander, I should know better by now, after all that's what got the ball rolling on this escapade in the first place.

Usually a restless sleeper, I'm now sleeping extremely well providing I don't give free rein to my imagination, and I'm confident my plan, or maybe I should at least be honest with myself and acknowledge it as my scheme, will work. It's strange but those of us known for being a smidgen stubborn, of which I grudgingly admit to at times, are not used to things falling into place so easily. Struggling and fighting for what we want is more familiar to us so it's a wonderful experience to discover everything doesn't have to be fraught with battles and sieges. To my detriment it's taken me a lifetime to discover this but finally my mind has chosen to view life from a different perspective, and I'm continually being made aware of the benefits of this inlightened insight.

It's 'D' day minus one and on this last day before departure I spend time completing a list of chores. Quick dead heading of garden blooms, advising my good friend and neighbour Maureen I'll be away for a few days, and last minute packing consume the morning hours leaving me late afternoon onwards to decide which village will be my first destination. I've narrowed the selection down to two small towns but still waffle over the most favourable, although they're not far apart as the crow flies. It's the day I'll cast off my comfortable, safe, and what has become a totally boring lifestyle and seek my first night's rest under a stranger's roof. All accomplished under the disguise of a somewhat slightly dubious interpretation of the English language. What a beautiful language it is. Even we who have spoken it for aeons, can sometimes barely understand each other if we venture beyond a ten mile radius. How many others can boast of this I ask you?

Evening finds me sitting in a now very tidy garden with what has become a companionable glass of wine and, without thought or judgement, feel such contentment to do nothing but enjoy the flowers and blooming shrubs. I still have not decided on my first destination and time is running out. Neither must be close enough to home that it's likely I'll be recognized, nor too far away to create a transportation issue. Once I've had the opportunity to hone my presentation skills I'll travel further afield, but until then I deem it wise to use prudence in my selection of holiday venues.

Watching a Wood Pigeon slakes his thirst from the bird bath, while his mate perches on the fence waiting her turn, I recall a village bordering the North Yorkshire Moors. Memories of the few B&B that catered to walkers and, considering the smallness of the village quite a fair size hotel, gives me food for thought. I definitely wouldn't consider a B&B for my purpose. A financial loss to them would be very harsh and worst of all such a personal attack on their generous hospitality. Unlike the hotel which probably overcharges for meagre services and would prefer empty rooms rather than shelter a weary traveller at a reduced rate; well now that was something different.

Wine finished, decision made, and bidding good-night to the world at large, I make my way to bed to lay my head on familiar pillows. To-morrow will find me taking my ease in another bed in another town. As I close my eyes I can't help but shiver in anticipation and excitement at the thought that I am on the precipice of a new jumping off point in life; maybe the final test to determine who or what I am. As if to place the seal of approval on my leap into the unknown I'm filled with feelings of empowerment. I can do it, I can succeed, I know I can. This is the final conformation I've been expecting and waiting for. Not only am I willing to accept the challenge, but I'm confident I'm up to it too.

Chapter Four

To-day promises to be long and tiring but as long as I arrive at my destination before dusk I'm confident it will be well worth the early start. After making coffee, sandwiches, and having a good breakfast, I've begun my journey before my bus pass allows for free transportation but willingly pay half fare to my first transfer point in exchange for the extra daylight hours. I'm the sole passenger at this time of morning and the bus driver is only happy to have someone to chat with. I tell him a little of my trip, minus my plans for accommodation, and he reminisces of his youthful walking trips on the moors. Soon he picks up other passengers and we cease conversation but the opportunity to discuss my trip has brought everything into focus and I realize, not for the first time, how I miss sharing life with someone. Oh well, I tell myself, now is not the time to sit on the pity pot so get over it, and I think about my first stop and change of buses.

I have a twenty minute wait for my next bus, the perfect chance to visit the loo and get a breath of fresh air. There is a lot of hustle and bustle at the station and a bit of grumbling too as those on their way to work, realize they're going to be late. An announcement of delay that causes stress to others is in my favour. I anticipated a longer wait till off peak travel came into effect but by the time we depart I'll be able to use my pass and save on any further outlay of cash today

* * *

Having finally arrived at Northallerton with plenty of time to spare I breathe a sigh of relief. I was well aware that if I missed this very important connection it would mean having to spend the night in town and an outlay of my very meagre cash reserve. It all added to the fact that while the day has been exciting, it has been stressful too. So much so that I haven't been able to eat my sandwiches or drink my coffee. Now though, anticipating my final transfer of the day, I realize I'm not only thirsty but ravenously hungry. Bumping along country roads I decide is not the time to spill coffee and strew crumbs so prudently decide to wait till I reach my 'holiday' home to satisfy my appetite.

Fifty minutes after boarding the last bus of the day I arrive at my destination, a lovely village quite removed from the regular tourist trade. Standing at the crossroads of the high street brings me up short. I now recall there is nowhere to avail myself of enough privacy to tidy up before presenting myself at the hotel. My only choice is to arrive dishevelled or go to one the pubs and use their facilities, accepting that I'll have to pay for half a pint so as not to draw attention to myself.

The tea time crowd of walkers have all but taken over the pub. As they wolf down plates of food piled high with the daily special, there is the friendly hum of camaraderie between mouthfuls, reliving the day's events and sharing favourite remedies for blisters. The sound of food sizzling mixed with tempting aromas wafting from the kitchen reminds me again of my hunger and thirst. At the moment amidst the bustle, I have gone unnoticed so forgo a pint in favour of searching out the ladies. Once located I unobtrusively as possible make my way towards it and minutes later emerge feeling surprisingly fresher for the quick splash of tepid water on my face and general tidy up of my person. Cape sitting casually on my shoulders and slouch hat adjusted to a jaunty angle, I hold my head high and feel my confidence return as I walk out into the fresh air to make my way up the high street towards the hotel.

A flighty looking young thing, obviously obsessed with her latest fingernail polish, appears to be on duty and as I approach the front desk she greets me with, 'just a mo I'll get Richard.' Scampering off behind 'staff only' doors she vanishes and is shortly replaced by a very good looking young man. Unfortunately as soon as he opens his mouth I know I have a problem

'Do you want something?'

Oh no, this is my worst nightmare, he think I'm a bag lady.

'Yes young man, I certainly do want something. Right now I wish to converse with the manager. Will you summon him or her, at your earliest convenience of course?'

The lad's mouth dropped open and he stands as if impaled.

'Wah, I mean what can I do to help, is something wrong?'

'Yes assistant manager Richard,' I say, reading his name badge, 'I think you could say there is definitely something wrong and I mean to correct it as soon as possible, comprendez?'

'No, I mean yes, I mean can you tell me what you want?'

'I believe I have already tried to do that,' I said sensing my control of the situation, 'I obviously need the manager not an assistant.'

'Sorry Miss, uh Mrs, er Madam, I'm new at the job and it won't look good if I have to call the manager on his day off, besides I'd really like to help you.'

I couldn't continue this way even if my nights rest was on the line; feeling sorry for him I tempered my uppity remarks and superior tone of voice. 'Well maybe you can handle this,' I said, looking him straight in the eye to convince him I was confident he could. Whereupon I handed him my business card and went into my rehearsed spiel. When I paused for breath Richard looked to his young co-worker enquiringly, possibly hoping for support, but she was studying her fingernails again, only now as if she'd just discovered them for the first time.

'Uhh I don't really know what to do,' he said, looking to me for guidance.

'Well Richard, if you've been put in charge then you are in charge and the decision is yours, wouldn't you agree?'

'I guess so, when you put it that way,' he responded.

'No, no lad, it's not how I put it, it's the way it is, is it not?'

'Yes Madam, you're right,' he agreed, as I cocked an eyebrow from beneath my slouch hat, grey Heron feather quivering in anticipation of a possible necessary, frantic, flight from this unexpected and unnerving situation.

Taut to the point of cramping, my stilted, robot like, legs followed in Richard's wake as he escorted me to a room with double bed and wide screen telly. Pointing out the room's facilities and breakfast menu he left me to my solitude. After securely bolting the door I exhaled a sigh of relief and flopped on the bed. Well girl you did it I muttered to myself, you haven't lost your touch. Damn, I was thoroughly drained and just needed some down time to process the day's events. This is when I most felt age working against me. Don't get me wrong, an accumulation of years have their advantages too. For example, bluffing your way out of sticky situations with a piercing gaze whilst holding your head high and mentally challenging anyone to dare defy you. Now that I recall, it worked well when I was younger too.

Just as I was about to disrobe, preparatory to dining on my less than fresh cheese sandwiches and probably by now just barely lukewarm coffee, a soft knock on the door stopped me in mid button. 'Yes,' I acknowledged, clutching my blouse front, prepared to meet the local bobby with his truncheon and handcuffs at the ready.

'It's Richard,' answered the caller, 'I have a tray for you.'

Going to the door and unlocking it I was shocked to see Richard holding a fully laden tray with a selection of nicely cut sandwiches, biscuits, cheese, glass of white wine and a carafe of coffee.

'Oh Richard,' I said, 'how thoughtful of you. After such a long day's travel all I really wanted was to stay in my room and relax. You've gone beyond the requirements of your duties. It is so very much appreciated and while I'm not supposed to give any verbal indications of approval until I submit my written report, I simply cannot possibly ignore this gesture of welcome and goodwill. It is most certainly acknowledged with gratitude and will not be forgotten'

As I closed the door on Richard's glowing face I admit to feeling a twinge of guilt at my deceit but it didn't last for long. The sandwiches and enticing aroma of fresh brewed coffee overpowered further mental recriminations and I tucked into it all. A hot shower concluded the day and snuggling down between clean, crisp sheets I let my mind wander. Finally it's over I told myself, the first day is a done deal and though it's been stressful it's also been damn exciting. So much so that even then I didn't know I was already half asleep.

Chapter Five

Next morning I woke long after sunrise. I must have been shattered to sleep so late. As I showered I began to realize just how stressed out I had been. Deceit has never been one of my high suits and I guess it rankled whether I wanted to admit it or not. Get a grip I told myself, you're committed for at least three days so deal with it. Mental pep talk over, I towelled dry and began to anticipate breakfast. In spite of the after hours sumptuous snack I was ravenous. Taking my checklist form with me to reinforce my façade, I made my way to the dining room. Half a dozen people occupying two tables are all that remain of the breakfast crowd. All looked up and acknowledged my arrival with bland smiles and nods of heads before returning to the contents on their plates. Hotel guests had reservation cards on their tables and the numbers corresponded with room numbers so it was just a case of matching your room number to the designated table. Once seated I was immediately approached by a new young face, such a pretty girl who asked if I wished tea or coffee. Upon my reply she whisked off and on her return with carafe in hand, she enquired whether I'd be ordering a vegetarian breakfast. Reassuring her not, I placed my order. Carley was her name and she was not only knowledgeable about the menu but proud to tell me where the food was produced and how it was cooked. Throughout breakfast she was attentive without being intrusive. I wondered if the management knew what a treasure they had in her.

After advising Richard I would be gone for the day and not require an afternoon meal, I strolled to the bus stop, intent on visiting Northallerton. The bus is on time and as I board reach for my pass only to realize it is not in my usual outside pocket. Reassuring the driver that it must be in my handbag, I sit down and franticly begin disgorging tissues, mints, maps and schedules, but there is no sign of the pass.

'So very sorry,' I tell the driver, 'I seem to have misplaced my pass. I used it yesterday when I arrived but can't find it now.'

'That's alright luv I remember you, take a seat and if you can't find it I'll call the office when we get to town to see what can be done.'

Sitting down I begin to shake. What am I going to do if I can't get a replacement? How will I manage, what if, what if? I'm on the verge of tears and tell the driver in a quivering voice I must get a replacement pass or I won't even be able to return home. My voice cracks and as the tears begin to flow I quickly reach for the now shredded tissues lying in my lap. The driver slowed down and glancing my way said, 'don't worry luv, just enjoy the ride, we'll have you sorted in no time.'

Trying to regain my composure I again apologize for causing such a fuss and sat quietly for the rest of the journey. As we reach the town centre the driver directs me to a café telling me to get a cup of tea and wait till he does some checking. When I explain I best not spend my meagre reserve of cash and will wait for him on the street, he extracts two pounds from his pocket and again points me in the direction of the café.

The tea did revive my fallen spirits and slowly I began to think clearly, keeping further panic at bay. It's not the end of the world I tell myself, it's only a slight blip and if worse comes to worst you'll have to forgo any more days away and use the cash you have for transport home. Somewhat reassured I finished the tea just in time to look up and see my bus driver entering the café. Waiting expectantly but with more hope than conviction in my heart, I'm overjoyed with relief as he hands me my precious document. It had been found and turned in earlier this morning by a passenger on his way to work.

Yesterday, on the last bus to my destination, while taking my seat I had attempted to slip the pass into the outside pocket of my cape. It had missed the pocket opening and fallen, lying just out of my sight. This morning, when the next passenger approached the seat I had occupied, my pass was in their line of view. On exiting the bus they handed it over to their driver and now it had been handed back to me. Thankfully peace and harmony have been restored to my world, for the present at least. In hindsight I have to admit, had I not been so intent on the fraudulent spiel for my grand entrance to the hotel, I would have realized my pass had not reached its destination and all this unnecessary upset would have been avoided, mea culpa.

My relief was apparent not only to my benefactor but to the patrons of the café also. As they applauded him for his Good Samaritan deed, this burly bus driver's face flushed like a small boy receiving a reward. When I insisted on returning his two pounds he agreed only if I promised to put the rocky start behind me and enjoy my holiday; something he was going to do at the end of his shift. I thanked him profusely wishing him a wonderful vacation filled with sunny days and also a promise. In his name I would pass on his good deed to someone else. I can't remember when I first started making these promises but like random acts of kindness, I've come to believe it changes people; both the giver and the recipient.

It was the market first, then on to a whole new array of charity shops, awaiting my discovery. I was on my feet all day, not stopping once since that cup of tea in the café. The sun was shining and it was a wonderful opportunity to explore and discover the local life. An unexpected bonus was the town's largest church was holding a craft fair and social. Stalls filled to overflowing with handmade garments for children, home baked goods, and an assortment of whatever else could bring in some badly needed pounds for church repairs. Mostly I browsed, being conscious of my minimal funds, but couldn't resist buying a daily journal offered at fifty pence, thinking I'd record my adventures so I would have some interesting reading when I reached my golden years. Raffle tickets were enthusiastically flogged by the teenagers of the parish, the prize a huge household hamper. I couldn't ignore their fervent sales pitch and purchased three for a pound, giving Richard's name and address as the owner of the ticket. I'd watched too many detective shows to fall into the trap of being tracked down because of an innocent slip. I think I'm becoming slightly paranoid. What makes me think I'd win anyway? Think logical old girl or you'll become a nutter I tell myself, and stuff the ticket stub deep into my pocket.

So as unsettling as the morning began it had blossomed into a fantastic adventure. By the time I boarded the bus back to the hotel I was exhausted, and thoroughly convinced I had exhausted all Northallerton had to offer as well. Entering my hotel room and glancing about as one does after a day out, I noticed fresh flowers had been placed on the night table. Nothing ostentatious, a few daisies surrounded with a bit of greenery. I smiled to myself as I gathered up clean clothes and went to have a quick shower before going to the dining room. There were about a dozen seated for dinner when I entered the room. Nice subdued atmosphere with soft background music and the low hum of conversation, it felt very pleasant. Carley appeared with the menu and a thoughtful enquiry of how I spent my day. We chatted a bit before she went off to bring me some wine while I decided on my order. Surprisingly I was not as hungry as I imagined. The excitement and pleasure of the day seemed to appease my appetite. When Carley returned I ordered a cheese selection with biscuits and fruit, saying I wanted an early night so shouldn't eat too heavy. I experienced such a feeling of calm as I sipped the chilled wine and nibbled at the cheese and fruit plate. An ordinary market in an ordinary town and yet I'd had a wonderful time. Now at days end I was tired but relaxed; enjoying the luxury of not dining alone while not being obliged to converse, it allowed me the pleasure of re living the day's events.

More diners are arriving so I decide to go to my room and read. Oops, I'd forgotten to bring my check list, I'm getting careless. Quickly I get out a pen and notepad and as I do so I notice Richard glancing my way. I give him a friendly smile and wave before bending my head to the task of writing a supposed report. Dumb woman, I chastise myself, ignoring details can blow your cover so stay focussed.

Chapter Six

Once again I've slept late and very peacefully. To-day is my last chance to explore so I want to make the most of it. Showered and fully dressed for the day with check list in hand, I confidently walk down the hallway and make my way to the dining room. Carley, cheerful as always, wishes me a good morning, pours my coffee and takes my breakfast order to the kitchen. Between sips of coffee I put my pen to paper and begin to compose my personal comments on the suitability of the hotel for my imaginary tourists. Just as I finish the rough draft Richard appears with a piping hot plate of the full English. No time to let this get cold and I tuck in; but not before I let Richard sneak a furtive glance at the written page and then, as though realizing my error, I snatch it from his eyes and turn it over, all the while smiling shyly as though asking forgiveness. Sometimes I shock even myself; when and where did I learn these nasty wiles?

To-day I'm going to Whitby. I love this small bit of England and as if to give approval of my visit, the weather predictions are perfect for spending a day by the seashore. I told Richard I would once again be gone till the evening so lunch would not be necessary. Really felt a twinge of guilt when he offered a packed lunch which I graciously refused, while thanking him profusely for his thoughtfulness. Whitby town means fish and chips and greasy lips, basking in the sun watching children have fun, and admiring those dive bombing rogue seagulls, not so lovingly referred to by Canadians as 'shit hawks.'

The town itself hasn't changed much since I last sat on it's beach to watch children building sand castles Busy as always, tourist are attracted to the abbey with their wild imaginings of Dracula, while the seafront offers a trip on a small replica of the bark Endeavour; including a few shrieks from landlubbers if the sea deems it fit to produce a wave or two.

Locals complain of, 'all these damn people milling about,' but lower their voices and paste on a smile as the same offer hard earned pounds. Everything is available from iced lollies to the tantalizing smoked kippers once publicized by that wonderful duo of Two Fat Ladies fame, Clarissa and Jennifer. Add to this the numerous shops offering the famous Jet jewellery and others, selling British souvenirs made in China, and you have a sea side extravaganza to remember.

Had I been able to choose an ideal day it would be today. The fish and chips were hot and greasy with lots of extra crunchy batter- bits crowning the top of the cardboard dish. Later the warm sun coaxes rich ice-cream to drip down the coronet to cling and ooze between my fingers; recreating a childhood aversion and causing me to rush towards the cleansing waves. The abrasive sand sticks between my toes and scours shoe calloused heels as I sink downward, at each step forward, till at last near the shoreline, I submerge my hands in a rock formed font, and all traces of the day are baptised in the vast sea. As I shake my hands dry and gather my belongings, I'm aware this most perfect of days is not only almost over, but can never be experienced again in the same way. I can't help but feel a deep sense of sadness and loss for moments like this, yet I also feel gratitude. Leaving the sandy beach there's also gratitude for the brisk wind that dries unbidden tears. Dries tears before they have a chance to trace salty lines down sun flushed cheeks and draw attention to this solitary woman, looking longingly at children playing as wave after foamy wave swirls about their spindly legs Listening too, as childish voices and high pitched shrieks of laughter echo in her ears before they are whipped far out to sea, to be lost forever but for the memories.

With the tingling sensation of a slightly sunburnt face, the taste of sea salt on my lips and grease on my breath I, like a graceless adolescent, slouch and let my body fold and meld into the contours of the bus seat. Closing my eyes I try to quiet my mind as it continues to dart about here and there. Finally I settle and spend the remainder of the trip back to the hotel mulling over the last three days and what I've learned. No matter if you want to or not, you learn something from every interaction and with every situation. It's just a case of choosing, as the lessons are always there for the taking. And once again I ponder my willingness to avail myself of the lessons offered these past days. To-morrow I go home with mixed feelings of what I've done. Damn it anyway, why a guilty conscience now? Bugger it I'll think about it later, or never, whichever comes first.

Arriving back at the hotel I notice the dining room is still busy with late evening diners In spite of having to present myself in very casual beach wear, I'm conscious of the necessity of an early night so forego the usual before dinner shower and head straight to my table. Once seated I remove a pen and slightly grubby, and more than a little wrinkled form from my handbag. Placing these beside my cutlery I eagerly study the menu. Even though I had breakfast and lunch I realize the sea air has given me a lusty appetite. Once again it's Carley that arrives to take my order and recommends the Lamb Henry. Enthusiastically agreeing with her selection, I ask only that the starter be substituted for a pint of John Smith. Waiting for my pint I relive the day's events until a basket of warm bread and yellow butter is placed before me along with my beer. Enticed by the yeasty, fragrance I generously slather sweet butter on bite size portions of the crusty loaf and resume my musings, savouring each morsel between sips of frothy bitter.

With plenty of time to work on the report before dinner I set my mind to rating the basics. All items appropriate to my stay are checked off, followed by a personal glowing recommendation to senior visitors wanting to experience small town English life. I'll copy this to a clean form before retiring for the night and present it to Richard on my departure. Once again my conscience twinges over my deception. How is Richard going to feel when he discovers he's been taken in by a woman older than his Mother? Is it going to colour his view of all seniors, will he become disillusioned and turn to a life of crime, maybe an axe murderer? Will I be responsible for his downfall? Bloody hell, why did I think I could pull off a stunt like this anyway?

After a reasonable night's sleep I looked over my rewritten report, sign it as Ms A.G. Mows, my pseudonym, and slip it and my business card into a hotel envelope addressed to the manager. I don't seal it because I could see no reason Richard shouldn't read it first. Besides, it mighty supply him with pre- warned ammunition to ward off a termination of employment should his manager be totally unreasonable. Let's face it, as manager, the man should have known the lad was not experienced enough to thwart wily women and the like. Hopefully, the experience would not discourage Richard from continuing with his much improved high quality service in the hotel industry. My final recommendation was that I personally thought he was more than capable of succeeding in any business enterprise he chose.

Entering the dining room which was almost filled to capacity with a tour bus group, I slipped into my usual chair and ordered a hearty breakfast. To-day was going to be long and tiring because my late start would affect bus connections and I wouldn't arrive home till after dark.

Richard was helping out in the kitchen, taking orders, serving, answering the phone and dealing with special issues. Special requests, if within the host's ability to provide, are never considered unreasonable, but during meal service it is generally frowned upon by establishments with limited resources. There was very little that could not wait till a more appropriate interval but the time it took to explain that tactfully would tax the patience of a saint. Richard seemed to be taking it all in stride and once again I was greatly impressed by his change of attitude. In the past few days it had become increasingly obvious that at some point this young man had been well trained and taught the rudiments to be a professional service provider. My appearance on the scene had obviously sparked a memory, now manifested in his renewed professionalism. What I couldn't quite fathom was what had happened to have made him forget his training in the first place?

After breakfast I returned to my room and gathered up my luggage, being very careful to check I hadn't forgotten any incriminating personal items that could lead to my identity. With everything accounted for I gave a fond farewell glance to my holiday home and closed the door. Stopping at the desk to leave my keys and the written appraisal of my stay, I glanced into the dining room making eye contact with Richard. Oh no, this was not going to be easy and I felt that old heart flutter again. Surprisingly Richard only smiled and as I indicated I was leaving my key and envelope he nodded in the affirmative, continuing to place steaming plates of food in front of hungry guests.

I didn't know if Richard expected me to wait for a final word with him but I can tell you I was only too glad to get to the bus stop. Not just because I'd made my getaway without the Mounties being called but mostly because I didn't want to look Richard in the eye and keep up my pretence any longer. Don't misunderstand, this is not the last time I'll do this but, it doesn't mean I have to enjoy everything that is necessary to accomplish my goal.

Chapter Seven

Long after dark, once again lying between crisp, fresh air scented sheets, having re- read my journal entries I think about the past three days. Granted I'm tired but at the same time rejuvenated, glad to be home but anticipating another trip. The only fly in the ointment is my conscience. I can't honestly say I'm proud of myself and what I've done. No matter how I attempt to justify my behaviour I come up lacking. And now as if to confirm my guilt, I begin to wonder if there is something I can do to compensate for my questionable actions. Hmm, I'll think on it, to-morrow. My last memory before I fall asleep is I'm sure I'll not only think of it to-morrow but for many more days after.

Morning arrives and I'm pleasantly pleased to discover the police have not broken down the door, taken me off shackled in handcuffs nor threatened to beat me with a rubber hosepipe. In fact I slept very well. Now with elbows perched high and cup in hand, I hover over my morning coffee like a hawk with wings spread, shielding the captured quarry. The time has come to make some important decisions that will effect my future. I've always played by the rules and it does go against the grain to discard them now. Damn, if I'm going to continue I'm going to have to find a happy medium between easing my conscience and being a high class scammer. I'm going to have to discover a way of somehow justifying the means to the end, a weighty problem to say the least. Again I remind myself to have another think on it, a bit later.

* * *

Thus comes an end to my first experience as a traveller. Instead of dusting useless souvenirs I choose to relive pleasure filled memories. The luxury of a comfortable bed, savouring again the incredible artery clogging but scrumptious full English breakfast. Reminiscing of brilliant conversations and exchanging Mensa calibre quips with with the most compatible of people, all gratis. Combine this with three wonderful days and nights enjoying views of Roseberry Topping, Captain Cook's monument and the wonderful Carlton Hills; along with day trips to Northallerton and the most hauntingly picturesque village of Whitby forever imprinted on my soul, I ask, how much better can it get? Not earth shattering you say? Well for me it doesn't get any better. Without wishing on a star I discovered my wish was within reach, so stretching forth my hand I grasped it and my wish came true. And in my book that's the best it can get.

As an afterthought and in hindsight I have almost convinced myself I did not just take from the hotel but did contribute something towards my stay. Richard's English improved considerably. He no longer greeted guests with, 'do you want something?' Instead he had miraculously reinstated his professional demeanour including a neater appearance and welcoming smile. Not to boast nor take undue credit but I do feel I encouraged him and enhanced his chances for further advancement in the tourist industry. Regardless of what his manager says and does on his return from Spain, Richard is in a far more employable position than before I arrived. The only downside to this is it may be a good thing, much hinges on the manager's opinion of Richard's decision making skills. More hindsight, have I just discovered a means to justify my behaviour?

Because I couldn't resist the opportunity to find out if Carley was still employed at the hotel, three weeks after returning home I made a phone call and asked to speak to her. Thanks to a chatty reception desk temp I was happy to learn Carley has already moved on to bigger and better things. On my last night as a guest, after I'd finished my wonderful lamb dinner, the couple seated next to me struck up a conversation and we chatted till our pudding arrived. During the short conversation I remarked on Carley's outstanding qualities as a service provider. They told me they had certainly noticed and had already inquired if she had ever considered working in the tourist industry. Receiving a positive reply they agreed to pass on her interest and their recommendations to a friend. Subsequently, Carley is now in the process of becoming a fully trained tour guide in Whitby. She loves her prospects and by next year will be fully engaged during the summer months as a guide, with the added option of learning about advertising and promotion in the tourist trade during off season. Financially rewarding also, even though still a trainee, she is earning more than she realized from working at the hotel. Not surprising she hasn't severed all ties and is still in touch with Richard. Can't help thinking it would be nice if something developed between those two. Wonder if they realize how well matched they are? Thanks to same chatty temp discovered Richard's father is not only manager but also the owner of the hotel, so while his son may have got a good telling off, it was unlikely he would have been be sacked. All has ended without undue tears so they say but something niggling away at the back of my mind, still refusing to show itself, tells me I've not heard the last of it yet.

While the next four weeks find me resuming former habits, not everything is the same pre 'H' day. My outlook has changed. I wake up with a renewed energy and always with the unspoken expectation that this may be the day I decide to become a traveller again. The weather in the past week has topped up the water butt and watered the garden well enough for weeds to outstrip flowers. Thankfully today's early morning hours are bathed in warm sunshine heralding the promise of fine weather for the next week or so. Kneeling in the sweet smelling grass still damp from the abundant rainfall, I pull weeds and cast away all negative thoughts as quickly as I dispose of those thriving unwelcome guests to my flower patch.

Somehow and for whatever reason, the idea of going back to North Yorkshire seems a good idea and immediately the name of Thirsk comes to mind. Now where did that come from I ask myself, I hadn't thought of that small village in ages. I'd been there a few years ago, just a stopover on a holiday to the Coast. Still employed at the time, my schedule was limited so was unable to do the area justice. The townspeople were friendly and I felt very comfortable in the village. I remember thinking I would like to return for a longer stay that would enable me to explore the surrounding countryside also. Now with time restrictions no longer an issue, maybe I could return to Thirsk, use it as a home base and venture forth on daily side trips of discovery and adventure. 'Ah ha that's it!' I shout aloud then quickly glance about to make sure no one's heard me talking to myself. There were other advantages to this plan. I'd know my way around and could even revisit the market in Northallerton. This is what I've been waiting for, I know it I tell myself, and go back to weeding and thinking and pondering and planning. I grudgingly force myself to work in the garden till late afternoon. I was eager to go inside and even start packing, but common sense told me to sort out the garden first, then I'd be free to devote all my time to my next exciting adventure.

After a shower and dinner from my horde of surprises in the freezer, I began to think seriously in terms of schedules. My journey time would be a little less than before but it would still be to my advantage to leave home early. It was vitally important that I arrive in plenty of time to reach my new holiday home before dark. The excitement was building with each new thought. I remembered the area being larger than my first host town and because of its association with the author James Herriot it drew more tourists. I saw this as a definite positive as I would be less likely to put myself in a position to attract attention. However it was much more than that, having a successful trip behind me had done much to increase my confidence.

I decided to use my original list to set the house in order and make plans for when I would break free again to meet the new challenge. Clothes weren't a problem this time but I had an urge to revisit the generous, hippy lady's little shop to return the drawstring pouch. To-morrow would be a good day to do that so with the decision made I settled in for the evening.

Later sitting in bed with map in hand, once again I begin to experience a gentle fluttering in my chest. Just the anticipation of embarking on my secret life once more is enough to cause my heart to race, but this time I'm confident it's not an impending heart attack just sheer enthusiasm.

The trip to the footballer's town again took well over an hour but unlike my last visit, time was not a concern as there was nothing I absolutely needed. I had set aside the whole day and even included plans to enjoy a budget priced lunch to celebrate yesterday's decision. I easily found the hippy lady's little shop but to my dismay it was closed. A note pasted to the door said she wouldn't be long but it didn't say from when. For all I knew it could have been put up yesterday. Disappointed, I walked back to the high street and checked out the other charity shops. It wasn't a waste of time because I found a nice leather folder and thought how much better this would look than just walking around the hotel with a sheet of paper in my hand, so much more business-like. It was only £2 and looked new. I also bought a small tube of expensive hand cream for 50 pence. Purchases all but lost in my voluminous, cloth, shopping bag, I wandered back to see if the hippy lady had re opened her shop. Still no sign of her so returning once more to the high street I made a check of the bus schedule. As usual I'd just missed a bus so a cup of coffee would serve to not only revive me but also pass the time. I realized I was quite disappointed not to have met up with the shop owner so decided I wouldn't bother with the planned for lunch but settle for a scone. I entered a busy tea shop and after paying for my order glanced about for a vacant seat. The waving hand caught my eye and there sat the hippy lady enthusiastically beckoning me to her table. 'Oh, I'm so glad to see you I didn't know when you'd return to the shop,' I said, placing my tray on the table.

Gesturing for me to sit she replied, 'most people know where to find me if I'm not open but you're new to town aren't you?'

'Yes, I was here for the first time a few weeks ago and when I unpacked my bags I found something of yours that had got mixed in with my purchases.'

'Can't imagine what that could be,' she said, sipping her tea.

As I extracted the cotton pouch from my handbag she looked surprised and said, 'Oh that, you didn't want it?'

'No I quit smoking a long time ago and wouldn't dream of starting again.'

'Hmm, yes I see, guess I misjudged, sorry if I've offended.'

I thought the conversation had taken a funny turn but didn't quite understand why and looked at her in puzzlement. She was also aware communication had failed to make a connection and returning my gaze said, Do you know what kind of tobacco this is?'

Continuing to stare, I searched her face for a clue as to what had gone awry; then the reason for her question finally penetrated my dull awareness.

'Ah ha, no it didn't register but it does now,' and I promptly burst out laughing in embarrassment at my own stupidity. She began to laugh too saying obviously I wasn't the only one who had missed the mark. During the next hour we finally got around to introducing ourselves and becoming acquainted. When it was time for Daisy, for that was her name, to reopen her shop she encouraged me to return with her and see if there was anything that I fancied. I found a little book of verse I liked and was told it was mine for the asking. When I insisted on paying Daisy said if it eased my mind I could drop a donation into the hospice tin that sat at the end of the counter.

With a few minutes to wait for the bus I had time to reflect on my day. What a truly captivating person Daisy is. Daisy, the perfect name for someone of her attributes, and so likened to the qualities of that flower. Capable of withstanding fierce winds by bending, thereby not breaking. How I wish I had learned that earlier in my life. In my travel journal, the one I'm writing to entertain myself in old age, I'm going to include anyone that has anything to do with my adventures. This definitely includes Daisy and my impression and admiration of her.

Two days later I'm up early, sandwiches and flask packed, house locked up and waiting at the shelter for my transportation to arrive. Like my first trip I paid half fare to take an early bus and by 9:30, was ready to board a connecting bus for the first of my transfers which allowed me to travel free. Although still morning the day was already showing signs of becoming warmer than usual so I carried my cape rather than wear it and put my hat with the elegant grey, silky heron feather into a carrier bag. I looked a bit more casual but knew the exchange for comfort was well worth it. Besides, it took no time at all to throw the outdated cape over my shoulders and don the slouch brim hat.

Transformed in an instant to the mysterious femme fatale of yesteryear, or maybe yester-never would be more accurate.

It was mid-afternoon when we pulled into a town offering frequent transfer service to my next bus so I chose to take a break at this point in favour of a late lunch, recalling my previous hunger and thirst towards the end of a days travel without having had either. For forty-five minutes I sat in a quiet church yard enjoying my home packed cheese and onion sandwich and sipping almost hot coffee, all the while contemplating my life so far and my future. It seems the older I get the more prone I am to reviewing my life, where I had wanted to go, how far I've come and mulling over the discrepancy without becoming maudlin and morose. I choose churchyards not because of their significance to the final place we rest our heads but because they are peaceful and quiet and I can give free rein to my thoughts. To-day I'm thinking it's becomes increasingly difficult to divorce ourselves from many of the day's distractions, to allow for the all important time necessary to renew our spirit and energy. We wonder why we feel depleted, drained, exhausted. We accuse our bodies of creating aches and pains, tormenting us even in our sleep. We go from doctor to doctor beseeching them to, 'fix me fix me.' Could it be that we ourselves have neglected the attention necessary to care for our spirit life, allowing the sacred energy to become shrivelled to the point of dysfunction? The end result causing at least some of our misery of both body and soul; misery that once addressed would allow the healing of our spirit and restore our lost energy. Medical doctors demonstrate their service of love by healing our bodies of many things but it is unreasonable to expect them to heal our souls too, they have their own to care for. Attention to our soul is our own personal job and we avoid it, every chance we get. Ah well, more of these thoughts are best left for another day. Right now I remove all traces of having sat amongst past peers on this warm North Yorkshire day and return to the bus terminal. Two more transfers and I'm there. It's been a good journey, pleasant travelling companions, cheerful drivers and best of all, the excitement is still building.

Chapter Eight

Destination reached I once again search in vain for a public lavatory. After numerous enquiries I'm advised by a local shopper to try the small tourist office. Pleasant lady on duty showed me to their staff room and within a few minutes all traces of travel are erased. Fresh lipstick applied, cape draped casually over my arm and hat carefully held in hand, I decline the offer of a much needed cup of tea as I give my thanks for their welcoming hospitality. I'm very anxious to be on my way because of something I've just been made aware of. While repairing my appearance I overheard a phone enquiry regarding accommodation and learned that a new guest house had recently opened on the edge of town. Eavesdropping further I learned the proprietor was new to the business but seemed very pleasant and would surely welcome any last minute guests. Made to measure I thought, and once obtaining directions, started the short walk to the house.

As I approached the massive front door I knew this had once been a home of distinction. The overall exterior of the building was quite imposing and upon entering the foyer I could immediately sense the ambience usually associated with the old fashion style of luxury. This was definitely a guest house and not your ordinary little B&B. Tapping the bell to summon the manager my imagination began to soar in wild flights of fancy. Dismal thoughts of tragic circumstances flooded my mind. Were once wealthy owners now reduced to letting rooms in their family home in order to avoid the equivalent of the workhouse? I hoped they weren't an ancient and decrepit couple trying to scrape together a few extra pence to subsidize their pensions. I knew I wouldn't be able to carry out my plan if this was the case.

In less time than it took to think another thought, my mind was shocked back to reality by the appearance of a most unlikely host, entering from behind a beautifully carved wooden door. Bearing no resemblance to my imaginary ancient, arthritic pair, he was grubby, unshaven and looked as though he'd been up all night. Greeting me with, 'ya want a room do ya luv?'

'Well now, that entirely depends on whether you're in charge,' I said, giving him my most haughty and disdainful look while drawing myself up to my full five feet three and a half inches.

'Yea, I'm the boss luv, now what can I do for ya?'

'Well sir it may be that I can do something for you and at the same time correct your obviously lacking charm in overseeing this establishment.'

Damn, that temper of mine was getting the upper hand, I need to calm down I thought, and took a deep breath as I tried to paste on a smile that didn't look like a grimace.

'Ooh, the grand lady is it now,' was his comeback, only looking slightly unsettled as he spoke.

'My good man, I can't believe you are in charge and suggest you get the manager at once,' I said, secretly preparing to flee if he showed any signs of removing himself from behind the reception desk and approaching me.

I seemed to have got through to him at last and looking a bit sheepish he said, 'sorry you're right, I'm in a foul mood, can we start again?'

'Well if you're sincerely interested in what I have to offer we might,' I said. Hopefully conveying that in the interest of mutual understanding I'd give a little too. Extracting my business card from my new leather folder and offering it to him, I began my spiel.

Twenty minutes later found me cosseted in a clean and extremely spacious room. The wonderfully high ceiling added to the old world elegance and enhanced the ornate carved embellishments that coupled the ceiling to the walls. This had to be one of the most elaborate areas in the house I thought as I familiarized myself with the room. Before long I had finished unpacking and left the room to descend the beautiful staircase to the foyer. The previously unshaven manager had since managed a quick shave and now greeted me wearing a clean shirt. I enquired about meal times and Leonard, 'call me Leo,' apologized that the kitchen was closed for the night but offered to get me a take a way. Refusing his offer but not wishing to seem churlish, I did accept a bottle of cold beer from his fridge. It helped to wash down the remains of the 'best before' cheese sandwiches I'd made early that morning, thereby allowing me to go to sleep dreaming of to-morrows grand breakfast.

Chapter Nine

I wasn't sure what roused me from sleep nor even when I'd become aware I was awake. It was ever so subtle but finally I became conscious of the change of state from sleep to awareness. The beckoning bird song drifting through the open window attracted my attention and I threw back the duvet and left my warm bed. I knew it would mean a long day if I didn't go back to sleep but the ensuing chorus could not be denied. Standing at the open window I breathe in the sweet scented morning air. Bright flowering vines catch and dazzle my eyes. Hypnotically lured I follow their wispy, fragile, tendrils clutching at brick work, attempting to drag themselves towards unattainable chimney pots, declaring supremacy over all. The verdant lawns still damp with dew glistened as morning sun let down its warmth to drive the last hazy, mist skyward. It was too much to ignore. Wrapping myself in a coverlet I descended the staircase and let myself out the great front door to wandered unobserved, exploring the garden. Wild rabbits scampered away at my intrusion, blackbirds and thrush halted in their search of juicy grubs. What a glorious morning! Nature was pulling out all the stops to entice me to remain for further revelations. Sadly the human condition presented a stronger enticement, reminding me of my need for food and drink.

Leo had said the dining room opened at eight so just a few minutes past the hour I presented myself. There were five other tables occupied by a couple at each. Evidently everyone wanted an early start and Leo was going from table to table pouring tea and coffee. A side board held dry cereals, fresh fruit, a selection of juices and a variety of healthy snack bars. It was a pleasant room capable of serving at least twenty people. The menu was extensive and I wondered how many people it took working in the kitchen to accommodate the vast choices. I wasn't long before I had my answer.

After greeting everyone formally Leo announced that because of unforeseen circumstances the menu was somewhat limited. A substantial reduction would be credited to everybody's bill and he hoped his sincere apologies would be accepted. Only one older couple seemed to think this was a catastrophe but after a few filthy glances from the other diners they decided to cease grumbling and accept what couldn't be changed. Leo put on some background music and it served to lighten the mood of the unsettling beginning. When he came to take my order I said coffee was fine for now and giving me a grateful look he nipped back to the kitchen.

Everything was progressing fine until the male member of the disgruntled couple insisted his poached egg was too hard. Leo apologized and as he removed the plate to replace the offending egg, it slid onto the lap of the man's wife. Hysterical shrieks reverberated throughout the dining room. The couple stood and announced they were leaving and had no intention of paying anything for the abusive treatment they had received. Everyone was shocked at their behaviour and smiled understandingly at Leo, who stood as though cemented to the spot.

'Leo,' I said, 'let me give you a hand.'

Grasping his elbow and gesturing towards the kitchen door he, like an obedient child led the way. There was no sign of any kitchen help, Leo had being doing it all.

Understandable under the circumstances, the kitchen was in more than a bit of a shambles. I quickly turned off the smoking grill just in time to rescue the bacon and sausages from becoming overly well done and asked Leo what needed attention first. He seemed to snap out of his daze and told me how many guests were waiting for breakfast and, adapting ourselves to each other's work rhythm, between the two of us we finished cooking and plating up the remaining meals without further delay. Later as guests sat enjoying a second cup of coffee, there were smiles all round. In spite of the lack of kitchen staff the quality of Leo's food was excellent and the set-up of the kitchen had been designed for efficiency.

Now having returned to the dining room to have my own breakfast, which I'd cooked to enable Leo get on with things, I was chatting with the diners when the pleasant morning was again interrupted by a commotion, this time coming from the front desk. Leo had gone to try and make amends to the disgruntled older couple but to no avail. I could hear him say that of course they wouldn't be charged for breakfast but there was no reason they should not be held accountable for their room charges. Voices were raised and getting louder. Then the young couple I had been chatting with looked at each other and nodded. Excusing themselves they rose from the table and exited the room. Within moments their voices could be heard to the exclusion of all others as the two of them in turn, proceeded to give the complainers a dressing down that would have made a judge proud. Finally silence, shortly followed by the sound of the huge front door closing. The justice seeking young couple returned to the dining room and their table. The room was unusually quiet as all of us waited for news of the outcome of the altercation. Surprisingly the young crusaders were oblivious to our curiosity and seemed intent only on finishing their coffee. A few moments later Leo entered and as I looked at him questioningly, the unnatural quiet of the room was shattered by a burst of applause as he held out his hand displaying the cash. At once everyone spoke their mind, offering an opinion on the brilliant resolution of the situation.

Gradually the room cleared as the diners left to begin their day till finally only Leo and I remained. Topping up our coffee cups he said, 'I guess this morning's service pretty much excludes me from your recommendation list.'

'No, not at all Leo, you handled a difficult situation very well and it could happen to anybody.'

Looking relieved he thanked me again for my help and took himself off to the kitchen to tidy up. The mornings are a busy time in the trade. After breakfast service and resulting clean up there are the bedrooms and other guest areas to deal with. Shopping for food, along with laundry and ironing fill in the afternoons, not to mention being available to take bookings at any time.

I left the house within the hour planning to spend the day enjoying the town, browsing in shops, getting a feel for the local life and just generally relaxing. To-morrow was market day in Northallerton and I was looking forward to that but for now my destination was a stop at the bakery to purchase a Cornish pasty baked in Yorkshire. Later I would search out the local churchyard to sit and enjoy my pasty lunch while the fallen crumbs would be eagerly consumed by chubby sparrows and their fellow foragers. It was then I would reminisce of sharing past lunches in like settings but as always, one in particular would stand out above all others. The beautiful and peaceful St. Mary's churchyard in Penzance, overlooking Mounts Bay. Who would have thought the simple act of sharing with the homely, sparrow served a dual purpose of satisfying the hungers of body and soul.

Leo didn't serve evening meals so after purchasing some cooked chicken and coleslaw for my dinner I returned to the house. The dining room complete with dishes and cutlery was available for use by the guests. It served as a deterrent to greasy foods being consumed in the bedrooms, thereby reducing the chance of hard to remove stains on linen. After a tidy up from the days outing I went downstairs to find I was the lone diner. Usually I had a book with me for just such a situation but to-night I'd forgotten so rather than return upstairs I didn't waste any time with dinner, thinking I'd go to my room as soon as I'd finished and watch some telly. I had almost eaten the last of the coleslaw when Leo appeared. After enquiring about my day he asked if I would like to join him in a complimentary glass of wine. There were only two couples and a single coming to-night so Leo was confident of to-morrows breakfast service. Nevertheless I offered assistance if required and could see a look of relief wash over his face as he replied, saying maybe if I didn't mind, I could take orders. So having agreed on the duty roster for the coming day we proceeded to have another glass of wine as we waited for his guests to arrive and check in. During the course of our conversation I asked Leo how he came to be so short handed in a house that needed more than one pair of hands to run. His face took on an expression of both hurt and defeat and as he began to tell his story, his voice became overwhelmed with emotion. It was patently obvious the burden of having someone to share his predicament was long overdue.

Leo and girlfriend Sharon, along with Leo's best mate Devon, had bought the house with the understanding Leo would put up the down payment and Sharon and Devon would contribute monthly payments towards the mortgage. Leo's on going contribution would be to run the house with local part time help and all would share expenses over and above the mortgage. Basically Sharon and Devon would become silent partners till they had invested as much as Leo's down payment then all would look at upgrading the partnership. It had seemed a good idea and everything had been fine for seven months until Sharon and Devon, the silent partners, became non- existent ones as well. Approaching Leo one Saturday night they confessed they had fallen in love and wanted out of their arrangement. They had found a legal loophole dissolving themselves from monetary obligations and as far as they were concerned, it was a done deal. Having so thoughtlessly informed Leo of their plans they added their best wishes that he would do well and should he ever be in Alicante, to be sure and look them up. Leo's voice cracked with the pain of remembering as he told me he had explained to them if they reneged on their part of the deal he would lose everything to the bank, reminding them he could never have got a mortgage without their agreeing to be contributors towards the monthly payments. At the end of it all nothing could dissuade them and they left. That was three months ago and only with help from other friends had Leo managed so far. Unfortunately it was only a temporary fix and it appeared he was going to have to sell to satisfy the bank. He also faced the risk of losing his entire investment if he couldn't make enough to meet the mortgage payments till the property was sold. It seemed while there was no shortage of guests requesting accommodation, Leo's problem was he didn't have ready cash to pay part time help and without help he couldn't take in extra guests.

Our conversation ceased abruptly at the sound of the arrival of the first of his expected lodgers. Wishing him a good-night I said I'd see him in the morning and went to my room. Lying in bed listening to the sounds of evening and watching the curtains catch the breeze wafting through the open windows, I went over Leo's dilemma. So much for trusted friends I thought, he won't be taken in like that again. Then I considered what I was doing to him. Another betrayal, just what he needed when he was at his lowest. I didn't sleep well that night and I knew why.

Next morning Leo said he had booked another couple after I retired so if I didn't object he would appreciate any help I was willing to offer. We agreed I'd take orders, serve and answer the phone leaving him to concentrate on cooking. Everyone arrived within minutes of each other so there was barely time to deal with each request before moving on to the next. Even so, the service went very smoothly and Leo even had time to come out and chat with each guest while they finished their coffee. His manner was sincere and pleasant and I could see his guests warm to his charm. He gave a very different impression than when I first met with him. When the dining room was empty Leo and I had breakfast together then cleared the tables. Excusing myself to get ready for market day Leo stopped me to ask if I would join him for dinner that night as a small repayment for my help. Thanking him I said I'd be happy to do so and agreed to come to the dining room at seven.

Walking to town to catch the bus to Northallerton, I refused to think of how this was all going to end. Certainly not the way I originally planned. Damn, why can't I just be like Sharon and Devon and not care? Damn, damn and double damn!

The stalls were set up and already bustling with townsfolk searching out bargains when I arrived. What had started as a warm day suddenly clouded over and I was glad I'd brought my cape along. Nevertheless clouds didn't cast their gloom on buyer or seller and the day felt festive even if it didn't look it. Raucous bargaining could be heard as vendors strove to offer the best prices for their merchandise, thereby eliminating their competitors. Each as experienced as the other, and each knowing the value of a glib tongue, they entertained all. Up and down both sides of each row of stalls, determined not to miss a thing, I revelled in the atmosphere and spent a perfect morning. Thrifty as ever, inspecting, pricing, and sampling everything offered, I finally bought a thick wedge of cheese and bunch of grapes for lunch. This still left me a comfortable cash reserve for the last minute purchase of a bottle of inexpensive white wine, punnet of strawberries, fresh baked sponge and pint of cream; my offering towards the evening meal.

Afternoon found me once again in the local churchyard with cheese, grapes, and my thoughts. After I'd satisfied my hunger with this simple lunch I enticed the small, trusting birds with crumbly bits of cheese. They happily sampled every morsel but when no more crumbs were in the offing, they soon departed. Time for me to move on also I thought and I spent the next hour or so strolling a path that clung precariously to the edge of the bubbling, brook, that meandered through town. Eventually I made my way back to the market square and shopped for my contributions to dinner. With plenty of time before my bus arrived I decided on a cup of tea so chose a shop just emptied of the late lunch crowd. Finding a clean table and having just sat down, I realized I'd left the separate carrier bag containing the strawberries on the counter where I'd placed it while paying my bill Rising and about to retrieve it I hesitated as a man approached, forgotten parcel extended towards me. Thanking him and apologizing for my carelessness, I took my seat again. Smiling as he took the table next to me he said he'd seen me at the market and almost bumped into me, remarking it was obvious I was completely engrossed in the sights and enjoying myself. Returning his pleasant smile I informed him it was one of my favourite ways to spend a day out.

'By the way, my name is Raymond,' he said, offering his hand.

'Nice to meet you Raymond, I'm Agnes,' only then realizing I'd given my real name.

'Do you live here Agnes or just visiting?' was his next enquiry.

Immediately I told myself, stay alert woman, keep your wits about you and don't give too much away.

'Oh just a short visit,' I answered, and sipped at my tea, determined to change the course of the conversation.

'Do you often come to the market?' I asked.

'No I don't live here either. I had a little business to take care of in town so I thought I'd take in the sights too. Like you I enjoy markets so this was a perfect opportunity to combine business with pleasure.'

'Oh and where is home for you?' I enquired sweetly. His answer brought on a bout of coughing and sputtering coupled with a crash as cup met saucer in my haste to cover my mouth. Wiping my lips and eyes I gasped another apology and looked for the nearest exit.

'Here, here,' he said, beginning to pat me on the back, 'you'll be fine, it just went down the wrong way.' Oh boy, you have no idea I thought to myself, deciding the best thing to do was end the conversation as soon as feasible and exit. The last thing I wanted was to meet up with anyone from my first 'holiday town.' How frustrating I thought, he seems so nice too.

Recovering my dignity I said, 'well Raymond I must get the bus back to Thirsk but it's been lovely speaking with you,' and offered my hand in farewell.

'Please Agnes, believe me, I'm not in the habit of asking a new acquaintance out but I would love to take you for dinner day after to-morrow if you're free. I can offer respectable references if it will entice you to say yes.'

Well what did you expect me to do? How could I refuse an invitation complete with referral if need be? Just because he came from a town I'd once visited didn't mean anything if I didn't let it mean anything. By that I mean if I kept my mouth shut and my wits about me there wouldn't be a problem. Agreeing to meet in two days, at my request in Thirsk's town square, I left to catch my bus, returning in time to get ready for dinner with my host.

Leo met me at the door looking distraught and overwhelmed. He had overbooked. At some point, turning an extra page of his daily journal, he had inadvertently made bookings for the week ahead. Confirming phone calls proved they were for this week and while there were enough rooms, more staff was needed to handle the extra guests.

'Look Leo, I'll work with you full time to-morrow and stay on an extra day so don't worry, we can handle it,' I said. He looked at me with such gratitude that I hated myself all over again. Telling him to forget to-nights planned dinner and placing my shopping in the fridge, I got him to check the freezer and cupboards for supplies and suggested we do everything we could to get a head start on the morning service. While he went to purchase extra supplies I made sure all the rooms were aired and ready.

Stopping only for a quick sandwich and glass of beer, by ten o'clock that night all the guests had checked in and we felt sure we could handle the morning crowd. We'd be in the kitchen at half six and be fully prepared for eight o'clock service. I gratefully took myself off to bed telling Leo again not to worry and just get a good night's sleep. Brave words I thought lying in bed, totally shattered by the day's events. This had been a very long day and I more than felt my age.

To make matters worse, my conscience was playing hell with my peace of mind. I won't deny I was elated after my first adventure but suddenly the realization of what I was doing and its impact on others was beyond anything I could have foreseen. I finally went to sleep but only after taking a good hard look at myself and deciding to change my ways before I did any real harm.

Morning came too soon. I was completely dragged out. That damn Victorian upbringing at the hands of my great grandmother was still playing havoc with my choice of leading a new life that ventured well beyond those strict, governing, decrees. I should have known it was too late to become somebody else. My only excuse was that those I loved most had used that knowledge to get what they wanted before discarding me; no longer useful, therefore no longer necessary. The hurt I'd felt at admitting the truth of this had been life changing. Past conversations with friends had come to mind and recollections of the looks on their faces as I'd related another incident of requests for help from my brood. Always with the excuse I wanted to do more for them than was ever done for me. Actually I remember saying I'd stand by them for anything short of murder and even then I wasn't sure I'd abandon them. Now of course I understood what those looks meant. How in friendship and caring they had tried to tactfully suggest that just maybe I was doing all the giving. At the end of the day, admitting I had no one to blame but myself, I also admitted that it certainly didn't give me the right to run amok and wreak my vengeance by taking advantage of others. With a firm resolve to mend my wicked ways I went downstairs and greeted Leo. I poured us both a coffee and together we got stuck in to the breakfast service.

The morning went by in a blur. As the last diner left the room we began the clean-up but Leo was frequently interrupted to attend to the reception desk for checkout payments. Those returning for another night required any amount of information on how to reach race courses, parks, and the like, so it was almost noon before we were free to tackle the bedrooms and common areas. Bed making is hard on the back and by three o'clock I was done in. Leo said he would vacuum and I should take a break. He didn't have to tell me twice and I gladly made my way to my room. The next thing I was aware of was a knocking on the door and someone calling, 'are you awake?'

Glancing at my watch I saw I'd been asleep for two hours. As I opened the door Leo entered, holding a tray with black coffee, glass of white wine and mini biscotti, a favourite biscuit of mine.

'Thought you'd like this before dinner Ms Mows,' he said.

'Oh Leo, you shouldn't have, I'm perfectly able to come downstairs.'

'I know but I'm cooking the dinner I'd planned for last night and wanted to surprise you.'

'Oh how exciting, and what time shall I present myself and may I inquire if we are dressing for dinner?'

'Dinner's served at seven o'clock and no, we're not dressing because I don't have any more clean dress shirts but will appear in an exquisite Primark T shirt.'

'Wonderful,' I replied, getting into the spirit of things, 'and would Chef object if I presented myself in dressing gown and slippers?'

'Perfect Madame, that way if we imbibe more than we should I can chuck you into your sack without compromising your reputation.'

We burst out in laughter, enjoying our own silliness. Sometime soon, maybe even to-night, I'm going to have a serious talk with Leo. Even now as we enjoy the moment, I can't help but wonder if after my confession we would ever laugh together again. I really like him and admired his courage and his willingness to go forward in spite of being betrayed by his closest and most trusted friends. Considering my recent behaviour what makes me think I have the right to try to convince him that people in general are good and trustworthy? Furthermore what makes me think my confession could possibly justify my actions, making everything better for him, because I've had a change of heart? It simply doesn't follow this is feasible and I feel my face flush hot and crimson with shame just at the thought of not only what I've done, but am still doing to him. This charade cannot continue.

The lodgers have been informed the normally open dining area is pre-booked to-night so would only be available till 6:45. I passed the last of them on the stairway and while they smile in recognition they did look somewhat askance at my unusual attire.

The table was set to perfection, smoothly ironed linen cloth, delicate china and fresh flowers. Everything complemented the crystal cut wine glasses and water goblets which reflected a candlelight prism from the freshly polished silver cutlery. This was definitely not a casual evening meal. I wondered how Leo had found time and energy to set a table of this standard and still cook a meal after a day of cleaning. Maybe we were the ones having a takeaway but even that would taste gourmet if consumed in this ambience. As Leo entered the dining room, greeting me in his whiter than white T shirt, red polka dot kerchief tied round his neck and a linen serviette draped over his forearm, it was everything I could do to refrain from loud guffaws.

'Will this suffice Madam?' he asked.

'Oh definitely,' I say, 'I wouldn't have it any other way.'

'Thank-you Madame and now I shall begin the service of a gourmet meal fit for a gourmand.' We both lost it at this point and burst out laughing, unable to keep up a posh pretence after remembering our day's early chores including scrubbing out loos together.

Leo filled our glasses with a sparkling wine and raising his, toasted the food and diners about to partake, a casual but most appropriate blessing for any meal. Sipping our wine we discussed to-morrow's breakfast service, agreeing to meet again at half six even though there were fewer plates to fill. Leo instinctively understood the value of spending personal time with guests. Granted their stay had to have met certain expectations but equally important was their moments of being recognized as individuals by their host. When Leo absented himself to retrieve our starters I silently rehearsed my planned confession of accountability. No matter how I look at it, I can't justify my behaviour and can only hope for the chance to make amends. I'll not spoil his dinner but I do want to make a clean breast of it to-night if possible and see what I can do to right a wrong.

Our starter was everything it should be and had there been nothing else I'd still have gone to bed happy. Prawn cocktail, an old standby to be sure but if you love it, you love it. The entrée was Lamb Henry, the most fantastic way to cook lamb shoulder; served with a rich, silky, smooth gravy atop a mountain of mash and accompanied by a side of mixed vegetables. We did imbibe a bit more wine between starter and dinner and after consuming desert of the cream filled sponge oozing sweet strawberries, our appetites were satiated.

Dinner finished and now sitting in the comfy lounge chairs enjoying a last cup of coffee I got ready to appease my conscience.

'Leo,' I began, 'there's something I have to tell you.'

Looking at me as though I was going to tell him another corny joke, he answered 'oh yes, pray do tell Madame'

That remark changed everything, stopping me in mid thought. My intentions were to make a clean breast of it all but now at the last minute I realized what an incredibly poor time I had chosen. Definitely not to-night, it had been a wonderful evening and I couldn't tarnish it with my tawdry confession. To add further to my shame, I was beginning to suspect my wanting to get it over with immediately was more about easing a guilty conscience than an honest admission that I deliberately chose to hurt another to benefit myself.

'Well if I'm not taking too many liberties I would like to suggest that for the present we forget the original reason I came. I would be more than willing to stay until you get things sorted with the bank and are in a position to engage permanent help.'

The colour drained from Leo's flushed face and he stared as though what I'd just said was beyond his comprehension. When he began to speak, his emotionally charged voice stuttered at first till he could form the words. 'Do you mean it, what about your job, you know I can't pay you much and, and…'

'Listen Leo, I'll explain all about my job another time but let's just say for now I was contemplating a change anyway.'

'Oh Ms Mows I know I could get on my feet with someone like you backing me and we do work well together don't we?'

So childlike, so trusting he is I thought as I answered, 'I certainly agree with that my boy but first off you must call me Agnes or Aggie, Ms Mows is much too formal for your loo cleaning partner.'

'That part's easy, but what would you expect for wages Aggie?'

'Why don't we continue with our present arrangement of a room and breakfast and maybe a pound or two at the end of the week if the budget allows.'

We spent a bit more time discussing details of the impact my presence would have and agreed to book ten guests each night and see how we managed. Offering evening meals was still out of the question for now but it was definitely in the future after we'd sorted out the finer details, along with hiring permanent staff. I could see his eyes were filling with tears so said 'come on lad, a last glass of wine to seal our new relationship.' Gratefully I thought Leo excused himself to get the wine. Returning a few minutes later, glasses filled and composure intact, we toasted each other before retiring to our rooms and private thoughts.

I was up early next morning after having slept surprisingly well. I suspect the reason for that had something to do with the feeling a burden had been lifted from my shoulders. There was still the knowledge that at some point I was going to have to come clean with Leo and tell him of my escapades but hopefully before then, I'd have proven myself worthy in his eyes. He was such a nice young man and while I confess a growing fondness for him it was more than that. I had such admiration that young though he was, he had not let heartbreak, break him.

Chapter Ten

To-night I was going to meet Raymond and hoped I could not only keep my eyes open, but be bubbly and interesting throughout the evening. After last night's celebration and to-days full shift I was as they say, knackered. Leo told me to have a lie down about three o'clock and I didn't have to be told twice. Just as my head touched the pillow I remembered my neighbour Maureen would be expecting me back. A short call reassured her I was well and would be grateful if she continued to keep watch on my house. Mission accomplished, I don't remembering even returning to the bedroom.

I woke to the sound of the alarm and after a quick shower, dressed in a pair of trousers and summer top. Taking a cardigan in case the evening got chilly I went down to the kitchen to get Leo's approval and while promising to behave myself and be in before midnight, heard the doorbell sound. Unbeknownst to me Leo had called a cab saying the fare would be his treat. Normally I'd have relished the walk but after what was to me a long day I was grateful. Agreeing to the cab but refusing his offer of paying the fare I explained his treat was the wanting to give, and that was what would be gratefully accepted and appreciated.

When we had more time I would explain my belief that a true gift is the 'wanting to give' and not necessarily what is actually offered and received. Life has taught me there is very little of material worth that can be given to a rich man. However, if the concept of 'wanting to give' is understood by both, then whether rich or poor, it is a true gift from the heart and the acceptance of such is one between equals. For myself I'd taken more than enough from Leo and didn't want any more sins on my conscience. To-night at least, I hoped to shut out thoughts of the dreaded day of when I would bare my soul and ask forgiveness

Arriving at our agreed meeting place I saw Raymond waiting and looking very smart in chino trousers, open necked sports shirt, and casual loafers. He too had brought a light weight jumper to ward off an evening's chill. Watching him walk forward to greet me, once again I had time to admire his warm, friendly smile. Obviously a man comfortable with his feelings, he grasped my hands in his to lean forward and press his cheek lightly against mine; not a proper hug but not a handshake either. Very appropriate for the way I was feeling and a great start to getting to know each other better. Directing me towards his waiting cab he said he'd booked a table at what I knew to be a highly rated restaurant. I was more than impressed with his choice and told him so, adding I didn't think someone satisfied with a quick cuppa at a market town tea shop would be familiar with such a posh restaurant. Another of my less than great observations. Needless to say, before the evening was out, I would not only experience great difficulty extracting my foot from my big mouth, but closing it too.

Once seated at our table conversation flowed as easily as the wine, of which I was careful not to consume too much. Raymond didn't overdo it either so both of us had just enough to think we were young again; but not that young. The food and service were outstanding. No wonder this establishment received so many gracious accolades. While my income certainly didn't allow for enjoying this level of cuisine, I was not ignorant of dining first class. During the evening I noticed while everyone received exceptional service, Raymond was clearly catered to. As we were sharing a tiramisu I asked Raymond what he'd done to deserve such pampering and he very nonchalantly replied, 'I pay their wages.' Not knowing how to respond, I didn't. Finally Raymond asked, 'have I shocked you?'

'No, no of course not,' I answered, 'I always keep company with high flyers.' At this point I felt I'd been made a fool of and stood about to leave.

'Sit down will you please,' he said in a somewhat authoritative, commanding, tone whereupon I obliged simply because I didn't know what else to do. 'So my lovely Ms Mows, you think it's alright to manipulate and take advantage of others but don't like it when it's done to you.'

'What do you mean, what have I done to you to be treated like this?'

'Oh nothing to me personally, but you didn't mind taking advantage of my son.'

'What are you talking about I hardly know you so what makes you think I know your son? How could I possibly take advantage of him?'

'Well from his description you seem to fit the bill very nicely.' While it was strictly coincidental I saw you in the market you attracted my attention immediately. There are very few women with Canadian accents wearing capes and slouch hats in this area.' I continued to stare, not comprehending anything he was saying.

'Agnes, you know my name is Raymond Gordon and I've told you I have a son named Richard. I can tell by the shocked look on your face you have no inkling of the connection but it's time you knew that I am the owner of the Gordon Hotel and my son Richard is assistant manager. Now does that ring a bell?'

MI5 and 6 were pounding at my door. I would be thrown in prison for the rest of my life. I would be subjected to brainwashing and grotesque torture. I would be strung up in the market square for all to ridicule and then finally thrown outside the town walls, my barely recognizable beaten body ravaged by wild dogs, forever forgotten to humanity.

'May I explain,' I ask in my most humble tone, not connived but heartfelt.

'I'd love to hear your explanation,' Raymond said, leaning back in his chair preparing to listen.

I told him everything, all of it, feelings of being used, manipulated and at the last when I most needed to feel wanted, discarded. I finished with a last defence summation that I had no idea my actions would have such an impact and while I didn't expect my behaviour to be excused, I did think I'd taught Richard something and set him on the right path. At last emotionally spent and very close to tears of relief at having finally unburdened myself, I awaited his verdict and sentence. Raymond had listened without showing any emotion or reaction so it was impossible for me to gauge the effect my words had on him. His eyes remained on me throughout my recitation but now he turned his head to signal the waiter to bring us more wine and coffee. As his eyes returned to scrutinize me again I inwardly felt myself shrivel. Why didn't he get on and have done with? I had nothing else to offer, no more explanations. I was ready to accept my fate, a very penitent woman humbly waiting chastisement.

Raymond remained silent as the drinks were placed before us and though I remained in limbo concerning my fate, my mind was churning. I had made a personal commitment to Leo and while I was in no position to barter, I was not going to abandon him no matter what Raymond's pronouncement.

'Raymond, no matter what you think of me I am not all bad. I planned to return and tell Richard what I had done and encourage him to get Carley back to help him run the hotel. My impression of her was she was an excellent people person and would always be there for him, which is what he so needs. What you need to know is since then I have met another young man attempting to run a business on his own after being dumped by his girlfriend and best mate. I agree you have every right to prosecute me and realize I'm in no position to ask for favours or leniency but I sincerely ask that you first come and decide for yourself if what I see in this other lad is a success story waiting to happen, or just someone in need of a helping hand. You also need to know that in spite of being at your mercy I have made a commitment, and I cannot nor will not renege on that commitment.'

It was now doubly hard to keep the tears at bay. At this least expected time of my life and under these most unlikely circumstances, I had unknowingly loosed the reins to a deeply hidden inner pain. As if in triumph at finding its self at last untethered, it began to gather a strength that threatened to take over my emotions completely. I was quickly losing control, feelings driven by the past hurts I'd ignored or refused to come to terms with at the time. The sad fact is some of life's hurts cannot be undone; and while it may take a lifetime to process, in the end you must finally embrace them as part of the person you've become. That inner awareness once realized is the healing balm. The refusal to allow your past hurts to create misery for another innocent is in fact your relief and release. What had happened recently to make me forget this? How had I fallen into a self- pity trap, allowing my pain to fester to the point I only cared about my hurts?

I couldn't read the expression on Raymond's face. He gestured to the waiter again, requesting that our sweaters be brought and a cab summonsed. Rising from his chair he said, 'I'll be right back Agnes, I just want to have a word with the chef and staff and thank them for our dinner.'

Gathering what little dignity I could under the dubious circumstances I said, 'please convey my thanks also, everything was wonderful and I've never tasted better nor been better served.' At this remark he smiled broadly, obviously proud of his establishment and staff. I was surprised that my praise had such an effect on him. I wouldn't have thought it would have any value after my disclosures. Maybe I wasn't going to spend the night in prison after all.

Leaving the restaurant Raymond draped my sweater over my shoulders just as the cab arrived. Conversation was stilted, inconsequential, small talk during the ride home. Once the cab pulled up in front of the house I asked Raymond if he'd come in for coffee and meet Leo.

'No, not to-night,' he answered, 'if Leo's asleep I don't want to disturb him. I'm sure he's got a full day to-morrow.'

'Raymond,' I said, feeling my throat tighten as I struggled to control my voice, 'what are you going to do? I'm not asking for myself but Leo has no one else to turn to right now and I don't want him to pay for my mistakes.' Tearing my eyes away from his face for fear I'd break down, I glanced forward and gazed into the rear view mirror and the driver's eyes. He was waiting patiently for instructions, making no motion to interrupt our conversation.

'Well Agnes,' said Raymond, 'I'm going to ask for your phone number so that I can call and make arrangements to take you to another market I think you'll enjoy.' I sat rigid, I had been braced to hear the worst and all I got was an invitation. Raymond got out of the cab, and asking the driver to wait reached for my hand and led me along the path to the front door of the house.

'Is this your idea of humour, to see me suffer before you pass sentence?' I said. Now my true nature was rising to the forefront. I'd accept what was due but I definitely would not grovel and best he damn well understand it here and now. I heard my breath quicken and felt my temples throbbing. To be honest I couldn't be sure my nostrils weren't flaring too. A less than elegant specimen of mature indignation ready to do battle, I must have been a sight. Raymond's solution to defusing what threatened to become a very intense situation was to say he had a wonderful evening and if I'd hurry up and give him my phone number he wouldn't keep the cab any longer. I gave him the number which he entered on his mobile and then was thanked for a lovely evening with an unexpected hug and kiss on the cheek before he returned to the car.

Once inside I quietly made my way upstairs. I could hear rhythmic snores coming from Leo's room and hoped his rest would not only fortify him for to-morrow's bookings but my disclosures too. I couldn't leave it any longer now that Raymond had entered the picture. Then to add more pressure there was Leo's meeting with the bank manager in two days. I thought it just might help his cause if he could say he had at least one employee that wouldn't be a drain on the budget. If ever in my life I wished I was rich, it was now. Unfortunately wishes are just that, fairy tales of magical thinking, fit only for children, far too fantastical for someone of my mature years.

Morning arrived and I had slept surprisingly well for all my late night-carousing and hell raising. That's what Leo called it as he prompted me to tell everything about my wild night on the town. When I told him where I'd dined he asked me if I was aware what a high class establishment it was and how he aspired to one day own a business of that repute? Clearly we were in full agreement regarding the Chapel and Chimes so I promised if he asked no more questions while we worked, I'd reveal all after dinner that night. Little did he know what I meant by 'all' or dinner might have been postponed indefinitely. In hindsight, how different am I than Leo, and what do I know about all or anything else for that matter? Somehow due to my wild machinations we had become an enmeshed unit, Leo, Richard, Raymond and at this point, maybe a soon to be imprisoned fraudster.

The rest of the day passed swiftly with housekeeping chores and bookings. Time spent on the initial welcome of guests and later seeing them off, needed the personal touch so Leo and I had agreed he would be available to take care of both while I carried on with whatever task was at hand. Once again by three o'clock I'd given my best. It was becoming a habit for me to have a nap before dinner and I looked forward to the time not only to rest my weary bones, but re organize and calm my mind as well. It had been some time since I'd had to answer to a work schedule and while feeling more than slightly drained at the end of the day, after a rest I was surprisingly re-energized.

Now thoroughly refreshed and ready to meet head on whatever effect my revelation might have on Leo, or so I thought, I went downstairs. Leo announced we were having a fish and chip dinner and he was off to the local takeaway. I went about setting our table in the kitchen to-night. The dining room would be occupied by guests and we neither wanted to intrude nor, barring an emergency, be disturbed either. Leo returned by the back door and quickly went about filling our plates to overflowing. The aroma of crispy chips and crunchy, grease glistening, battered fish filled the kitchen with memories of the sea shore. I opened a tin of beer for each of us and we fell to. At last, when not a morsel remained on either of our plates we sat back sipping our beer.

'So,' said Leo, 'tell me about last night.'

Taking a deep breath I began to speak. First telling him what I had to say was not about my evening out but of something I had shamefully done to him. A questioning look replaced his smile and as I hurriedly got on with my story Leo seem to assume a frozen state, saying nothing. Even when my silence made it obvious I'd emptied my heart and soul, he continued to say nothing, head bowed as in prayer. I endured the ominous emptiness in the room as long as I could and imploringly begged, 'Leo please say something.'

He slowly lifted his head and as I looked at him I saw feelings of devastation had transformed his face completely. His features were only a mask of what they had been earlier. Deliberately raising himself to his feet and pushing his chair back he stood, hovering over me, like a bird of prey waiting to pounce. He seemed to be waiting, waiting to summon strength, both physical and vocal strength, then the terrible timbre and depth of his despair filled the room. 'Christ almighty, what do you expect me to say?'

I actually felt the roar of his voice in my ears because it surrounded me like thunder, engulfing every square inch of space, reverberating off walls to block out all other sound. His voice totally engulfed and consumed the room and everything in it. There was only this moment in time, no other and I was in a state of shock, dumbfounded. I hadn't expected a pleasant response but this was beyond my wildest imaginings. Such unbelievable anger, no it was far beyond anger it was pure all consuming, uncontrollable rage, a rage totally focussed on me. The veins on his neck and brow stood out and throbbed in unison with his pulse, he was truly out of himself and beyond reasoning with.

Spinning around, his chair toppled sideways as the momentum of his body sent it crashing to the floor. Now seemingly oblivious of his surroundings he gazed about wildly as if searching, until he focussed on the back door and lumbered towards it. Before I could gather my wits, he was gone. I remained stunned, in a funk, having no idea what to do. Thankfully the guests in the dining room had departed so there would be no knocks on the door from police to investigate a disturbance. This is it my girl, you've finally bitten off more than you can chew, I thought. For the next hour I waited, hoping Leo would return. Certainly not to make amends but to inform me he'd have me shut up in prison till hell froze over.

As worried as I was about Leo's state of mind and what he might do I couldn't think of how I could ever be of any help to him now. He would see me as completely untrustworthy, just like Sharon and Devon. My mind was in a fog as it tried to recover from witnessing that act of an all-encompassing rage of someone I had thought of as having a gentle nature. Gradually my thinking cleared and as it did the mist lifted and I remembered Raymond had given me his mobile number, in case something unavoidable delayed our forthcoming dinner date. It was early yet and the worst I'd do would interrupt his evening plans, surely Leo's welfare was worth more than his quiet night at home. Not only that, I was desperate. I got Raymond's answering service and with the hope he was just screening calls I left a message for him to call back right away. Fifteen minutes later my phone rang and answering I heard the words, 'what's happened?' It was as if he knew I'd soon be looking to him for help and he'd been waiting for the inevitable call.

'Raymond, I'm sorry to bother you but I didn't know where else to turn. I had it out with Leo and told him the truth about me and he took it very badly.'

'What did you expect Agnes? No one likes to feel used let alone been made to look the fool.'

'Please Raymond punish me with your words at another time, right now I'm very worried about Leo and am not the least concerned with what you think of me. Leo's welfare is what is of importance.'

'So, you've truly come to your senses have you?'

'Yes, I bloody well have,' I shouted, 'and I don't need you to remind me of my previous bad behaviour. Are you or are you not going to help me find Leo?' I know my voice contained more than a hint of ultimatum but I was surely past caring about a high flyer that would leave his son in charge of a hotel he was clearly not capable of handling.

A moment of silence followed my outburst then, 'where are you now?'

'I'm at the house, are you coming or not?'

' I'll be there within the half hour.'

'Thank-you Raymond,' I said softly, but wasn't sure he heard as the hollowness of dead air came quicker than I would have liked. What did I expect, a moment of reassurance that all would be well? Not bloody likely!

I waited outside at the entrance and very shortly Raymond drove up. As I got in he said, 'do you have any ideas of where Leo might go?'

'No not really, our relationship was completely work related. A day ago I suggested we forget my original reason for visiting and that I stay on to help him get on his feet and see the business established. If the bank won't agree to him holding the mortgage independently of his long gone partners, he'll lose everything. I thought if he could guarantee he had one full time employee not requiring wages then they might rethink his situation and extend credit. If I had the funds I'd invest with Leo and see him through this down time but unfortunately my assets are time and the offer of free work.'

Raymond looked at me long and hard before speaking then said, 'what is the favourite local in town?'

'Well I guess that would be The Sin-Bin at the end of the high street.'

'Right, then we're off to The Sin-Bin.'

Within a few minutes we had driven to the pub, parked the car and were walking through the front door. Well named for the time out penalty box Canadian hockey players were banished to when they flaunted the rules of the game, it seemed to attract a few others that weren't adverse to flaunting rules also. The first thing that got your attention was the noise, absolute bedlam it was. Why anyone came here to relax was beyond me but in a far corner sitting alone, was our very drunken Leo. His raised glass was having difficulty finding his mouth and it was obvious it was beginning to tip and pour a bit sooner than he anticipated.

Raymond ushered me to an empty table nearby and told me to stay where I was for the moment. I watched him confidently approach the bar and after he'd paid for a half pint, made his way to Leo's table.

'Hi mate,' I heard him say, 'understand you've had a falling out with an older woman.'

'Who the hell are you and what the fuck do you want?' was the reply. Leo's head continued to bob and sway in an attempt to focus his eyes on the voice and find the rim of his glass at the same time. It was obvious his eyes couldn't keep up with the motion so he tried shutting them and concentrated on the voice.

'Just a friend of a friend who thought you could use a ride home so as no one will worry about you.'

'And why the hhhell do you think anybody would worry about a sucker like me, why don't you just piss off?'

Raymond's voice deepened and became authoritative as he said, 'Leo there are people that worry about you whether you believe it or not, but we're not going to debate that now. Finish your pint if you must and let's get you home. Have you forgotten you have a full house to-morrow?'

Magic words, Leo stood up and reaching for Raymond's arm he willingly accepted assistance. I walked out ahead of them both and stood by the car. I didn't know what reaction my presence would have on Leo but hoped our boy was so far gone he'd barely notice me. As Raymond folded the last of Leo's legs into the back seat, I silently took the front passenger seat.

Glancing at Raymond I said, 'thank-you for more than you'll ever know'

'It's alright Nessie, I'll receive my reward in heaven,' he said.

Damn him anyway I thought, no matter the circumstances he can't resist winding me up. Still, I can't deny he gets my attention.

Raymond saw Leo to his bed and as I spoke my sincere thanks again, he embraced me quickly saying 'we'll talk tomorrow.'

As quick as that he was out the door and gone, leaving me standing alone, feeling isolated, dreading what the dawn would bring for Leo and myself. Most of all I feared the impact it would have on our relationship, a relationship that had become so very dear to me.

Next morning I was in the kitchen at five, pretty sure what Leo's condition would be but not sure how he'd handle it. The coffee was made and bacon and sausage sizzled on the grill when he came through the kitchen door. Something resembling a mumbled good morning came from his direction and I quickly replied with a similar greeting. Pleasantries exchanged we began.

The atmosphere was strained to be sure but neither of us gave an inch, so service was as usual spot on. It certainly couldn't be said we didn't work well together as a team. As the last diner left the room Leo asked, 'would you like some breakfast?'

'Well, I don't mind if you'll join me.'

'Sure but think I'll just have bacon and dry toast, what about you?'

'That suits me fine,' I answered, and proceeded to make toast and pour out the coffee while Leo warmed up the last slices of bacon. Hurdle number one surmounted, we were communicating on a mature if not entirely friendly level at least.

After breakfast the morning's work hung over our heads so an unspoken agreement meant personal issues would be put on hold for the time being. To-morrow we had less bookings so whatever wasn't resolved to-day could be dealt with then. By mid- afternoon Leo looked as though he might collapse at any moment so it was my turn to say, 'I'll finish up, you have a lie down.' Seeing he was about to refuse I glared at him and to make sure he understood that it wasn't a request but an order said, 'look this situation is all my doing so just go will you?'

I don't think he had the stamina to argue and as he walked away his slumped shoulders betraying how beaten down he felt. I watched him mount the stairs to his bedroom without another word but, if truth be told I would have burst into tears had he put up the least resistance. I'd never intended to hurt anybody. Heaven knows it was the last thing I wanted. Somehow in my own pain I had become so self-absorbed in the injustices I felt had been meted out to me, I hadn't given a thought as to how my current behaviour was to have such far reaching effects on decent, ordinary people. Unable to use either youth nor immaturity as an excuse, while still unacceptable might have a least been understandable, I had failed on so many levels. No, at my age there was no excuse and now I was reaping the effects of my thoughtlessness. More pain for having caused such unnecessary hurt to people who didn't deserve it.

Everything was ready for our guests before check in time so I poured myself a cup of tea. Sitting at the kitchen table I wondered how I'd go about restoring Leo's faith in me when I heard footsteps approaching. The short nap had made a vast improvements in his appearance. I gestured towards the teapot and when he said nodded his head yes I began to pour from the pot and at the same time, pour from my heart. Our conversation culminated with only minimal interruptions throughout and by the time all guests were settled we had more or less sorted our relationship for the time being.

Neither of us had eaten since breakfast so I put a frozen lasagne in the microwave and set about doing up some garlic bread. While waiting for it to heat Leo said he would call Raymond and thank him for seeing him home, among other things. He was well aware his rash behaviour could have damaged his business but even more serious, should the bank learn of his indiscretion, there would most certainly be no chance of further credit. We'd had a long and stressful day so I suggested he wait till Raymond called us as he said he would. Leo, appearing somewhat relieved not to have to tackle anymore issues to-day, agreed. We left it at that and ate our meal in relative silence, both reflecting on a past tense twenty-four hours and glad it was almost at an end.

Lying in bed that night I said a prayer of thanks that while our relationship had taken a beating and would need some serious rebuilding of faith and trust, I was confident Leo and I were to remain friends. Raymond was very much in my thoughts also and as much as I'd like to see him, I had no choice but to make my next priority his son Richard. Unfortunately I didn't see his father being instrumental in easing the way for what would be a less than happy reunion.

Raymond did call next afternoon enquiring of Leo's health and asking if we'd resolved our issues. We spoke for a few more moments and I told him Leo wished to speak to him. I handed over the phone and went out to the garden to allow Leo some privacy. It was some time before the call was completed but when it was Leo joined me outside. 'I've tentatively accepted an invitation for you and me to have dinner with Raymond at his restaurant next week,' he said. 'If you don't want to go I'll let him know, otherwise we'll meet him there on Thursday night.'

'That's fine,' I agreed, 'did he say anything else?'

' Nope just that he was glad we'd sorted things and he wished me good luck with the bank.'

While sitting alone before Leo joined me I had began to ponder again, a feeling I had come to think of as a sign that trouble was not far behind.

'Leo,' I said, as we finished dinner that night, 'do you think you can manage without me for one day?'

'Sure, you must need a day off, sorry I didn't suggest it.'

'It's not so much a day off from working but I really need the time to straighten things out with Richard before I face his father again. If I travel by train and leave just after breakfast I could be back by early evening.'

'Fine,' said Leo, 'I'll book a cab to the station for you.'

'No please don't, I'd rather walk, I have some mental preparations to make and walking keeps me focussed.'

Agreeing on the morning schedule I went to my bed earlier than usual but didn't fall asleep till long after I heard Leo lock up for the night.

Chapter Eleven

The morning commuters had long since freed the station master from his most pressing duties. Promptly after issuing my ticket he tucked himself into an alcove as far removed from the counter as possible and cradled a well stewed mug of tea. Even as I pocketed my change he was sipping his brew from the chipped beaker, revelling in the hot steam that also served to clear his sinuses.

Standing alone on the quiet platform waiting for the ten twenty it was impossible to think about anything else but my upcoming trip. Not a trip I looked forward to but so very necessary for so many people. Thinking back I wondered again why in my wildest dreams I'd thought I could use other people and thoughtlessly discard them as if my actions would have no impact on their lives? Memories flooded back and I recalled the hurt I'd felt when it had been done to me. Me personally, so I of all people should have known better. I felt such sorrow and and regret at my latest behaviour but knew that none of what I was feeling could or would release me from my need to make amends.

Mid- afternoon found me rooted to the spot, standing exactly where I had stepped off the bus. Though frantic to have this ordeal over and done with, at this eleventh hour I seemed to have lost my way, my mind in limbo, detached from my body. Finally the realization came that I hadn't moved because I was shaking so much I couldn't move. Oh please, I begged my inner self, don't give way now, you can't fall apart in the middle of the street. My shoulders braced in anticipation of whatever punishment was to be rained down upon them and struggling to gain control, I pulled my handbag towards my middle, clenching my hands so tightly I could no longer feel them. Finally I prayed for whatever strength a forgiving God would offer a truly penitent child and after what seemed an eternity, was able to put one foot in front of the other. Like a weary soldier trudging forward on a death march I walked till I reached the entrance of the hotel. Get on with it I told myself. You brought this about and you need to deal with it. Still for all my brave self- talk I felt my heartbeat quicken and my brow dampen with perspiration as the tension of the morning reared its ugly head again.

Straight through the front door and facing the reception desk I was confronted by Richard, full on, not six feet away, bent over the reservation ledger. It was immediately apparent there was to be no delayed encounter. If I'd hoped for a deferred meeting, perhaps a summons from a staff member that his presence was required, thus allowing him time to prepare and maybe soften his demeanour, I was in for a rude and obviously unpleasant awakening. Looking up at my approach, that smile that could be so endearing and engaging was swiftly wiped from his handsome face, as though it had been slapped off. Recognizing me he spat out one word, making it sound like such a vile curse that I was afraid my legs would give way.

'You,' was all he said.

'Richard please, may I speak to you privately?' I asked.

'Why?' he bit off the word, his tone clearly a challenge I wasn't sure I could rise to. Oh dear, this was even worse than I'd imagined,

'Richard please,' I said, again almost cowering in shame to hear my voice border on begging.

Gazing down at me with a look of pure contempt he addressed me, 'I've got a bus load of tourists checking in within the hour, if you want to speak to me you'll have to wait.'

'Of course I'll wait,' I responded,' is there somewhere I can sit?'

'Sit wherever you like, just stay out of the way and don't talk to any of my customers,' was his cold reply.

I went outside and found a bench in the shade. I wanted to resolve this problem I had created but I had to be on the last bus to the rail station or be here overnight. With the present state of affairs, asking for a night's lodging at the hotel was definitely not an option.

The tour bus arrived ten minutes later and within the half hour the foyer was cleared of guests and luggage. Soon the large hotel doors swung open and Richard emerged, glanced around and strode to the bench where I was seated, sitting down as far away from me as he could.

'Well, let's hear it,' he said, his icy tone seething with power and control. The thought that nothing about this meeting was going to go well flashed into my mind and at this point I knew I had nothing to lose. That one thought was the much needed catalyst for recovery and feeling my wholeness return, I also found the strength to close off the ever draining mental state of guilt and remorse. Like closing a curtain to shut out the darkness of night I rallied an inner force I didn't know until now I possessed. Thus I began.

'Richard,' I said, my voice seething with a barely controlled steely calmness, 'if you don't get off that bloody high horse of yours I'm going to bloody well kick you off and them I'm going to bloody well kick your ass too!'

His eyes popped, his jaw dropped and his entire face was transformed into a mirrored portrait of shock. The ensuing extended silence was threatening, and it held me in in its grip till Richard began to laugh, and he laughed till there were tears in his eyes. Not seeing the humour of the situation but suspecting it was at my expense I stood about to leave in a huff until, at the last minute interpreting the look on Richards face, I surmised he believed I was about to make good my threat. Only then did the humour of the situation penetrate my overly emotional and slightly befuddled awareness. Like Richard, I finally grasped the absurdity of the situation and my feelings of helplessness vanished. Richard, laughter under control, took my arm and said, 'my dear Ms Mows please come in and join me in a glass of wine.'

I'd shocked myself as much as I had Richard so followed him inside without further argument. We sat down in the cool lounge and as Richard poured our wine remarked, 'Dad said you were feisty but he didn't tell it by half. Aren't you afraid of anything?'

'Yes Richard, I'm afraid of many things, and not the least, confronting you with my confession and a determination to make amends. I deceived you and used your youth and inexperience to defraud you. The bed and meals are nothing compared to what I stole from you in good faith and trust. This makes it almost unforgivable but still, I want to try to make amends. Right now I'm not sure how I'll be able to do that but don't want you to continue thinking you were taken advantage of because of your lack, believe me the lack was within me. I lost my way for a bit but I'm back on track now and mean to do my best by you.'

We finished the bottle of wine, had dinner and agreed to meet again. Richard booked a cab to take me to the rail station and by the time I reached Leo's house, though exhausted in body I was lighter in heart than I'd been for a long while. Now there was only Raymond to deal with, and oh dear God in heaven, that man was a match for anyone.

Unlocking the huge front door just before dark, I entered the foyer and noticed the dim light burning at the reception desk. Stopping to double check to-morrow's bookings and see if there had been any changes, I saw a note from Leo saying he was out for the evening and while to-morrow was an easy day, he had an appointment with the bank manager in the afternoon, so hoped I could manage the desk during his absence. Writing a big 'yes' at the end of his message I dragged my tired body up the stairs to my bedroom.

The morning hours went smoothly as expected and during the time Leo was away I had only to stay within hearing range of the phone. I prepared some vegetables for our dinner and had the rest of the afternoon to myself. I wished Raymond would call, I wanted to straighten things out with him and maybe, I admitted to myself, wanted to see him again too. Leo and I were joining him for dinner on Thursday but that wasn't the same as seeing him alone. I had just hung up the phone for a new booking next month when I heard Leo come in the back door.

'Leo,' I said anxiously, 'how did it go?'

'Right now I can't say Aggie, I have another appointment next week and they want you to come in too. Something about a firm agreement you'll stay on for a trial period. As for now, as long as I can pay the interest they'll carry me until they sort things out. They are trying to do whatever they can to help me stay in business and I can't ask for anything more than that.'

'Let's think positive Leo, I've got an idea or two myself if worse comes to worse but that hasn't happened yet and may never happen.'

Leo walked over to me and gave me a quick hug asking what I had in mind for dinner. In spite of our recent past tribulations this is where our relationship stood at the moment. Being open and honest with our feelings we knew we were risking betrayal again as we both struggled to rebuild our confidence in people. Smiling to myself as I bustled about the kitchen, my inward smile was for the happiness I felt at Leo's determination and mine to be willing to continue expressing our feelings for each other, proof to me we were up to the challenge.

* * *

Thursday evening Leo and I were dressed in our best and waiting outside for Raymond to pick us up. As the cab approached I could see there were two passengers and for a moment I thought Raymond had brought a date. As the cab door opened I breathed a sigh of relief as I recognized Richard. He indicated for Leo to take the seat next to him, allowing me to sit by his Dad. It was surprising how much alike they looked and I wondered why I hadn't seen it before. Raymond leaned over and gave me a quick kiss on the cheek and said how nice I looked and instead of coming back with a flippant quip I just thanked him as I buckled my seat belt. Oh dear I fear I am am becoming a softie, it must be all these men I'm spending so much time with.

Richard and Leo, after introductions, immediately began to talk shop so that left Raymond and I to our own devices. We were content with small talk and soon arrived at the restaurant. I could see Leo was anxious to get inside and see everything. Raymond had noticed also and suggested to Richard that he give Leo a tour of the kitchen and introduce him to the staff before dinner. Richard fairly beamed at the request and it was obvious to me Richard held his father in very high esteem. The two young men excused themselves and were out of sight before we were seated.

Raymond ordered wine and we sat sipping but not saying a great deal. I wondered if something had gone wrong so remarked to Raymond that he seemed very subdued tonight. 'I've had a lot to do this past week dealing with lawyers. When my wife walked out she wanted nothing but her freedom but now that the love of her life has left her, she's having second thoughts and wants half of everything I have left. I made her a cash settlement at the time of the divorce and that's binding but still she's looking for more.'

'Raymond, I'm so sorry and believe me I wasn't prying it's just that you did seem different.'

'I would have told you sooner or later Aggie, it's not a secret but I thought that part of my life was over and done with.'

'Does Richard see his Mother?' I questioned.

'No, he was very hurt at the way she treated us, he'll deal with it eventually but for now as far as he's concerned she doesn't exist.'

'And you, how do you feel about her?' I said, feeling I might be treading on tricky ground.

'She was part of my life for over twenty years but I have another life now and am content to keep it that way.'

Oh dear, I thought, does that mean he's off women for good? Not that I think I'd stand a chance with him but I guess there might have been some wishful thinking creeping into my thoughts. I thought he was about four or five years younger than me and knew men went for someone ten or more years younger than themselves so when I admit to wishful thinking what I really meant was my thoughts were bordering on pure fantasy.

'Anyway enough of the gloom and doom Aggie, we're out for a nice meal and some fun. I wanted the boys to meet because if they're agreeable I'm going to suggest something to them as a business venture. I've checked into Leo's background and he's everything you say he is and more.'

Just then Leo and Richard returned and I could tell by the flush on Leo's face he'd just visited his idea of heaven. 'You should just see it Aggie, it's everything a kitchen should be. Chef invited me to come in one day and give a hand with veg. prep so I'd get a feel for the pace of a busy kitchen. So far all my experience is at chef school and the few kitchens that took us on for work experience.'

'Richard, you must have visited the kitchen many times, what do you think of it?' I asked.

'Cuisine isn't my area of expertise or interest Aggie I love the business end of managing a hotel. The bookings, arranging tours, even doing the books is relaxing for me.' Raymond looked at me and smiled, we were both on the same page. No wonder after checking Leo's credentials he wanted the boys to meet.

Another bottle of wine was ordered along with our dinner. The meal was outstanding again and though Raymond and I drank sparingly the young men seemed to have never ending appetites for wine and food. They'd both thought having two deserts was the best choice because neither could decide on one. Our meal finished, Raymond told his son we were leaving and to get a cab for Leo and himself when they were ready, adding a fatherly reminder that tomorrow was a working day for both. Rising from our table, Raymond grasped my hand in his and led me to the kitchen and presented me to the staff. We both offered our thanks of appreciation for a fine meal and service and it was obvious that our approval was much valued. Chef Aidan took Raymond aside for a moment and though I heard Leo's name mentioned I didn't get the gist of the conversation. We waved good-night to the boys and walked outside to wait for our cab.

When we reached Leo's I asked Raymond if he'd like a nightcap so he paid the cabbie then called Richard to inform him to call for him at Leo's and he'd share the cab back to the hotel. We settled ourselves in the lounge and enjoyed the remaining half bottle of wine that Leo and I had opened before Raymond and Richard picked us up. Our conversation was mostly about the boys and their prospects till Raymond asked what my long term plans were.

'Well Raymond,' I said, 'I mean to stay long enough to see Leo on his feet. I want things sorted at the bank so there's no chance he'll lose his business. I'm aware his heart is in a kitchen but he thinks he can build a reputation through his guest house and when he has more experience can move on. His ambitions are not unrealistic and in spite of what's happened in his personal life and how it's affected his business prospects, he won't quit. While he was in a bit of a slump when I first met him I can tell you, he's an inspiration and fighter all the way.'

Raymond had a gentle, soft smile on his face as he leaned over and kissed me full on the lips. I wasn't expecting it but I wasn't taken aback either, it just was.

'Nessie,' he said slowly drawing away, 'I suspect Leo isn't the only one that's a fighter and an inspiration. Something tells me you recognize it in others because you have the ability to fight and inspire also. I don't know if you're aware of it but you shocked Richard back to reality. I left him in charge of the hotel hoping it would make him snap out of the negative attitude he'd developed after his Mother walked out. It's been more than three years and during that time Richard changed. He had been a trusting, loving man but he took his Mother's rejection too much to heart and became soured on life and women as well. He began to treat woman as though they would eventually turn on him so why bother showing them respect and kindness. Get what you can and dump them became his motto. The only woman that stuck by him was Carley, she knew what everyone else was seeing wasn't the real Richard. I think Carley and Richard will eventually become a couple because they've given each other space to grow. Hopefully when they meet up again and get to know each other on an adult level they'll realize it.'

'So Raymond, you've chosen your future daughter-in-law have you?'

'No, but maybe it wouldn't be such a bad idea. Come to think of it I haven't made such a bad job of choosing someone for me to get to know better have I?'

'I didn't know you'd made a choice or a decision,' I said.

'Ah, finally I know something the great Nessie doesn't know!' He laughed and kissed me again.

Raymond left with Richard when the cab dropped Leo off. I was glad I remembered Leo would soon be returning home or else I can't really say how the evening would have ended.

Next morning Leo was looking a little sheepish but after a cup of coffee and a gentle reminder from me that one must pay the piper, he got stuck in and the day went well. We were both optimistic that something would turn up. As long as I stayed we could manage enough bookings to pay the interest on the mortgage and expenses, provided we were frugal. Frugality was my speciality. I could make a pound work like a fiver and have change leftover so I began to teach Leo my idea of money management. Simple things like forgoing the convenience of pre packs of jam and marmalade and instead filling the servers from super market jars, same for using fresh milk for tea and coffee in bedrooms. Maybe most cost effective of all was coming to grips with our differences regarding breakfast waste. Leo served huge portions, not wanting to be found lacking, while I thought feeding the garbage bin was nothing short of sinful. Finally we reached a compromise. We agreed to ask guests whether they wanted one or two sausages instead of automatically serving two, same for bacon and eggs. I only got my way on this point after promising faithfully that if they chose two of anything I would not ask them how much weight they usually gained when on holiday. Small savings to be sure but each one put another pound in Leo's pocket and needless waste was stopped.

The meeting with the bank was fairly straightforward. They really did just want to meet me and be assured I would remain with Leo till he sorted things out. So far they hadn't made a decision as to the amount of credit they would be willing to extend but said he would be given adequate notice if the decision was not in his favour. Leo and I agreed they were being as fair as they could under the circumstances so decided we would remain optimistic till the last.

I phoned my neighbour Maureen and good friend that she is, reassured me it was not an inconvenience to forward any mail that looked important and do a bit of light gardening. I had done the same for her and her husband over the years and now that he'd passed away she was only too happy to feel needed and wanted again. I knew that feeling very well. Another reminder how everything returns to us in one way or another during our lifetime. When I realized and accepted this truth I grew more as a person than at any other time in my life. I think I was aware of this when I was a child but then forgot. The time it took to remember was not pleasant but eventually I did remember and for that I'm very grateful.

A week had passed and I hadn't heard from Raymond. The only reason I noticed was because, well you know, as usual I was missing him. I just bet he's trying to keep me dangling, I thought. I knew he was too damn good looking for his own good and now he's playing Mr hard to get. Well bugger him, who cares? I have quite enough to keep myself occupied without having to concern myself with the likes of him. And now tell me another I told myself.

Leo had gone out for the evening at my insistence. He'd kept his nose to the grindstone far too long without having time off to spend with his mates. Dressed in denims and white t shirt he reminded me of my own boys at that age. After giving me a good-bye hug at the door, I felt a surge of happiness watching him walk away to meet his friends. His jaunty stride touched my heart. To a stranger's eyes he was just a carefree lad without a worry in the world. To my knowing eyes he was a young man on the threshold of his future, excited, eager but now wary, and would never again be as vulnerable and trusting as he had been a few short months ago. Like me, Leo had learned the hard way.

Surprisingly I fell asleep before Leo came home and when I did wake next morning my first thought was did he get home alright? Sounds coming from the direction of his shower room reassured me and breathing a sigh of relief I went about getting ready for the breakfast service. Leo didn't look any the worse for the wear and said he'd had a good time. He also asked if I was free after dinner because he'd wanted my opinion on a few things. 'Oh my,' I said, 'this sounds serious I hope I'm up for it.'

The day carried on as usual as we went about our chores, chatting and sometimes laughing about the idiosyncrasies of past guests. Business was good and we continually had requests for more bookings than we could handle. It really bothered me that because of a temporary shortage of operating funds we had to turn down the chance for extra business. I was going to ask Leo if there was any chance the budget could stretch to extra help for two hours a day on an on call basis. Leo and I could deal with added guests at breakfast but we would need help with the bedrooms if we booked extra guests. I'd struck up friendly chats with Betty our next door neighbour and got the impression she had spare time on her hands and would welcome the chance to earn an extra pound or two. She didn't need the money to live on but would use it as an excuse to buy her granddaughter treats on their day out. The small amount we would pay her would be returned many times over at the increase in our bookings. I also thought this would be a plus for our side when Leo next met with the bank.

***

A fragrant bouquet of oregano, basil, garlic and mixed spices filled the kitchen and the crusty sour dough loaf wafted mouth-watering whiffs as I removed it from the oven. I'd told Leo I'd do dinner to-night and had decided on spaghetti and meat balls. With pasta bowls filled to overflowing with spaghetti drenched in tomato herb sauce, then generously topped with bite size meat balls and finally surrounded with chunky cuttings of garlic bread, we began our Italian feast. I had found some oversize kitchen towels to serve as bibs because this was a meal for slurping the long strands of whip like tomato coated pasta that splattered at will.

Leo pushed back his chair and groaned in pleasure, 'that was awesome, thank-you for a meal that would receive the seal of approval from any Italian Mama. I think you should be known as Grande Mama Nessa, you're a serious threat to them all.'

'I'm so glad you enjoyed it Leo but it doesn't make up for the wonderful meals you've cooked for me.'

'Given the right conditions I can do so much better Aggie, I know I can.'

'You'll get your chance before long Leo I know you will because you don't give up.'

'That's true I'm not going to take no for an answer no matter who says it,' he replied.

'Good,' I said, 'now let's discuss why you want my opinion.'

'Well, I know this might sound like a bit of a cheek but would you be willing to continue with our present arrangement if I hire someone else for a few hours, allowing me to take on more bookings?'

'Leo, you've been reading my mind, ' I exclaimed, 'are you thinking of anyone in particular?'

'No but I'll find someone if you agree'

'Agree, I not only agree but I think you've got the perfect employee living right next door.'

I then went on to tell him what I knew of Betty and why I thought she might be agreeable to our offer. Leo immediately went next door to make his propoasal to Betty. I could tell he'd been successful when his voice reverberated throughout the downstairs, mindless of his upstairs guests

'Aggie, Aggie where are you?'

His shouts from the foyer reached me in the kitchen, where I now sat. Having taken care of our dinner dishes and preparing the kitchen for morning service, I remained to enjoy a last cup of tea while waiting for Leo's return.

'Leo, lower your voice or you'll lose the guests we do have,' I admonished.

'She'll do it, she's happy to do it, she really wants to do it, and it's all thanks to you my Mama Nessa.' He pulled me out of my chair and swirled and twirled me about the kitchen floor, dancing in sheer delight and hugging me as though I'd given him the only thing he'd ever wanted. Once again I was reminded of how fortunate I was to still have Leo in my life after I'd treated him so badly, and silently vowed never to treat another human being as I had him, ever again.

Next morning Betty arrived at seven thirty to observe our routine and pitch in where she felt confident. She was a marvel and nothing seemed too much for her to try. The guests loved her and she'd more than earned her wages by nine thirty. Still she didn't leave, she wanted to know more. Over a cup of tea I let her know we couldn't afford to pay for more than two hours but she said that was fine, she'd stay to see how things were done and think of it as her training session. That said the three of us moved to bedroom detail and once again she kept up with us. It was close to noon and finally we had to insist Betty had completed all the training she would ever need. She'd earned her wages twice over and we did not want to take advantage of her generous nature. Our newest employee had seen and helped with it all: making beds, scrubbing out loos and showers, hoovering, dusting, laundry, kitchen clean up, she was utterly amazing. Leo could hardly wait till we were finished housekeeping so he could pop over for a quiet visit with Betty and reassure himself she'd return when required. It was an on call job and wouldn't suit everyone but when Leo returned he couldn't keep the smile off his face: it was a made to measure agreement for two nice people.

* * *

A soft tap on the door woke me fully from my usual afternoon nap. 'Nessa, Raymond's on the phone, he wants to speak to you.' Leo had taken to calling me Nessa now and I somehow had the feeling he really wanted to call me Mum but knew if I was right, he'd get around to it when he was ready. Handing me his mobile he left the room.

'Hello Raymond, how are you?'

'Fine Aggie, I've been busy and haven't had a chance to call but don't want you to think I've forgotten you.'

'No, no, not at all, to tell you the truth Leo and I have been snowed under and haven't had time to think of anything else but the house.'

'Are you free to-night Aggie do you have time to come for dinner?'

'Well I did tell Leo I'd man the phones while he goes to see a girl he's interested in but if you don't mind leftovers you're very welcome to have dinner here with me.'

'Now that's an invitation I won't refuse, what time shall I arrive?'

'Come about six and we'll eat at seven, I hope you like pasta.'

'Love it, I'll see you later then,' he said, as he rang off.

Now it was my turn to skip around the kitchen in happiness. Hanging up the phone I was stunned to think I had been able to come up with a reason for not jumping at the invitation. Raymond was used to being in charge and I didn't want him to think I was available at a moment's notice by appearing overly eager to see him, which of course I was. But now I had to drag Leo into my little deception so I told him the truth. His teasing smile said it all, so I gave him a look to say that if he wound me up, he may just live to regret it. He knew what the look meant and remained silent but wouldn't break eye contact till I openly threatened him in a tone that suggested dire consequences were about to be rained down on his head. Laughingly giving his word and promising he'd keep our secret he said he was more than happy to have an unexpected night off. He'd recently met a pretty girl serving pints at her Dad's pub and wanted to get to know her better so this was the perfect opportunity.

Dinner was easy to prepare. At my request Leo picked up some pastries and salad fixings so other than putting the salad together and making more garlic bread, it was only a case of setting the table and reheating the sauce while the spaghetti cooked. I didn't dress for dinner but did a mini makeover, making sure not to forget a dab of perfume, something I'd not used in a very long time. It wasn't only the sauce that I wanted Raymond to think smelled good. I swear the chemistry between men and women ever ends. Here I am almost sixty-five and thinking like a star struck twenty year old. Still it can't all be one sided I tell myself. With more than ample reason to avoid me he doesn't, and with no obvious reason to seek out my company he does. Granted I do have a vivid imagination but with regards to attraction between the sexes I'm pretty realistic. One doesn't usually think of peacocks and pigeons together but even arrayed in all its dazzling fluorescent finery the peacock has a shrill, high pitched scream while the slightly drab wood pigeon is capable of lulling squab and man alike

Raymond arrived just after six o'clock accompanied by a large bouquet of roses surrounded by a frothy frill of Babies-Breath. He'd also brought two bottles of wine, one white, the other red. Looking casual but so very smart in jeans and open necked sports shirt, I was at once conscious of the spicy scent of his aftershave as he leaned forward to kiss my cheek. Trying to keep my mind on arranging the roses in water, I spoke of Leo and his new interest in the publican's daughter. Finally, when there was no more to be said on the subject and with the damnable aftershave still permeating my nostrils, I succumbed to a glass of wine while continuing with the final preparations of our meal. I'd made up my mind not to indulge in more than one drink to-night and was already at my limit and the evening hadn't even begun. We were going to eat in the dining room and even though I'd arranged our place settings in close proximity, the overall appearance had looked a bit stilted and formal, even bordering on drab. Now because of the addition of flowers there was the suggestion of warmth and welcome and just a hint of the romantic. Earlier I had considered a random placing of tea lights on the crisp white tablecloth but for fear Raymond would think I'd staged an intimate dinner for his benefit, I resisted. Which brings me to where I am now. Denied the magnificence of more than one master craftsman, the beauty of a crystal cut vase filled with gloriously scented roses enhanced by flickering candlelight. Really, I silently question my earlier reasoning, just how could pasta ever be considered an intimate meal designed to flatter the male ego? Wild, endless, strings of pasta spraying tomato sauce everywhere and the ever present desire and need to slurp. Combine this with a frantic fluttering of mascara covered eyelashes, in futile attempts to dislodge a speck of oregano and it's more a setting for comedy.

Dinner was every bit as tasty as the night before and surprisingly for all my concern just as relaxed. When I donned my kitchen towel bib and then presented Raymond with his, he burst out laughing saying this was the proper way to eat spaghetti. We finished with pastries and discovering neither of us really appreciated red wine, I exchanged the bottle of red for one of Leo's whites and we shared another glass with our coffee.

Relaxing in the lounge we spoke of everything and nothing for a time. Then the conversation turned to Leo's dilemma. I told Raymond about hiring Betty and his opinion was we'd discovered a gold mine in her. I asked him based on his experience, what he thought Leo's chances were that the bank would refinance him. The look on Raymond's face was not encouraging. 'I can't say for sure Nessie,' there he goes again calling me Nessie, I'm sure he thinks of me in terms of the beast of the great Loch, 'but,' he continued, 'he should know before too much longer.' We were sitting side by side turned slightly to face each other as we spoke and I was increasingly aware of him and his after shave. He really was quite charming and it was becoming difficult not to concentrate on his mouth. His lips were very interesting, drawing my eye, and I had to admit I was thinking I wouldn't mind exploring them a little more. I don't know if he was reading my mind or just knew what I was feeling because without any warning he leaned forward and kissed me, a kiss that I wouldn't soon forget. His lips moved ever so smoothly, encouraging me, and I was not about to refuse. We were so in synch, so joined, so in touch, it was impossible not to yield to each other, until the memory of being used flashed into my mind. I had no idea why that particular thought came but immediately knew I wasn't going to fall into that trap again.

'Raymond, Raymond,' his breath and mine was not only audible but quickening in measure. He halted his caressing hands and looked at me enquiringly.

'What's wrong?'

'Sorry Raymond, in spite of my age having an affair is not, nor ever has been my style. I don't mean I've never been involved but I don't take it lightly.'

Pulling away from me he looked confused, 'what makes you think this is an affair and I'm taking it lightly?'

'Well what would you call it? You must have your pick of young, attractive woman so why would you choose me?'

'What is the matter with you woman? Yes I do have my pick of whom I wish to go with and so do you. Why do you think I wouldn't want to be with you?'

I was so taken aback that I sat staring at him, saying nothing.

'Well answer me will you? You've just accused me of trifling with you, if I may use an old fashioned word, so tell me why I wouldn't want to be with you?'

'I don't know, I just don't know and it scares me more than a little because I feel you're getting too close to me and it's frightening.'

'Nessie, you're a strange but exciting woman. No man would ever be bored with you because no man would ever know what you were going to come up with next. Has it not occurred to you I find that very attractive? You're unpredictable but still within the realm of normality.'

'Oh thank-you so very bloody much, I'm really chuffed that you consider me normal so bloody hell to you too.'

'I didn't say I thought you were normal, I said you fall within the range of normality.'

'You didn't say range you said realm,' I shot back.

Looking as though he was summoning all his patience Raymond grasped me by the shoulders and looked at me with such intensity that for the moment I was so taken aback that it seemed prudent to keep my thoughts to myself. 'Nessie,' he said, if you'll just shut-up for a minute I'll kiss you again.'

Thankfully Leo arrived home shortly after we'd made up and I was glad for that in more ways than one. I certainly did not want to be bested by any more of Raymond's smart arguing tactics. I'd discovered he could argue as well as any woman I'd crossed swords with and that's saying a lot.

Chapter Twelve

We were busy, as busy as we'd ever been and Betty made herself available whenever we needed her. She was a jewel and Leo and I made sure she knew how much she was appreciated. Betty and I were very different in nature but we seemed to have bonded. She confided to me how she thought she'd never have the chance to get to know her granddaughter Victoria, known as Tory, as her son and the child's mother weren't married. At the end of the day the woman was more interested in her own desires and happily signed over all parental rights to Betty's son Byron. Byron had eventually married a woman that welcomed his child as her own and made sure Betty was included in the little girl's life. If Betty had Tory stay overnight she would invite me for lunch or dinner, whatever suited my schedule best, and the three of us would end the day with a proper little girl's tea party. Tory called me Auntie Leo and happily sat on my lap if I agreed to read her nursery poems. She seemed to love the rhythm of the meter and memorised great volumes of verse after hearing it only once or twice. Betty and I firmly believed she was a child prodigy and laughed at our grandmotherly aged bias.

Three weeks after Leo's last bank visit he received a letter requesting he make an appointment with the powers that be. His first thought was he wanted to speak to Raymond but Raymond had returned to his hotel last week to take care of some pressing matters. I advised him to postpone making the appointment till I spoke with Raymond, saying I expected a call from him that night. After we had brought each other up to date on the past week, I told Raymond about the banks request for an appointment with Leo. Immediately he wanted to speak to Leo and as I handed over the phone to him I signalled I'd be at Betty's. We spent a pleasant hour sorting out the world's problems and agreed if the local government asked our opinion we'd sort them out soon enough too. Giving her a hug good-night I thanked her for the visit and said I'd see her in the morning.

I was surprised to see Raymond's car parked in front of the house when I returned. Entering the dining room I saw him and Leo hunched over the table looking at papers and deep in conversation. Both looked up and Raymond said 'we're almost finished Aggie, can you make us a cup of coffee?' Through the kitchen door I could hear the occasional word but not enough to get the gist of what they were saying. It must be about the upcoming bank appointment but I couldn't think what couldn't have been said on the phone that necessitated bringing Raymond to the house. Taking the coffee and cakes through it was obvious business was completed as now both men were sitting on the sofa in the lounge looking very pleased.

'So what have you two been up to that makes you look like the cat that stole the cream?'

'Raymond has come up with a plan and he's coming to the bank with me to present it.'

'Oh and what have you decided?' I asked.

'Well by no means does it solve the problem but it is a temporary solution to give Leo more time to make some decisions and implement them.'

I was puzzled, were they not going to tell any more than that? 'I see,' I said a bit frostily, 'and is there anything I should know about this new proposal?'

'Oh no Leo, we've ruffled her feathers and now she's going to be difficult,' said Raymond.

'My feathers are not ruffled as you so chauvinistically put it Mr Gordon, and if you prefer not to take me into your confidence than I shall bloody well take myself off to bed.' So saying I left the room only slightly slamming the door.

'Nessa, come back,' I heard Leo say, and then a muffled laugh from Raymond which made me want to slam my bedroom door too but because of the guests I didn't, just twisted the door knob as though it was Raymond's neck. Oh that bloody man, I thought to myself, I'd like to shake him till his teeth rattled, uppity bugger that he is. I was just getting into bed when there was a soft knock on the door,

'Aggie may I come in?'

'What do you want Mr big shot?' I replied.

'Aggie I'm coming in.'

'No you bloody well aren't, the door is locked.'

'Then open it damn quick before I knock it down and wake all your guests,' he threatened.

Grabbing my dressing gown and wrapping it around me I unlocked the door but blocked his entry.

'What is the matter with you woman, why are you so huffy?'

'Oh first it's ruffled feathers and now it's huffy, anything else you want to add before I shut the door?'

'Bugger this, sometimes you're impossible, I'll see you in the morning.'

He turned his back and went downstairs. Oh who cares? I thought to myself as I snuggled down in bed. An hour later, still wide awake and feeling confused I admitted to myself that I cared, and I cared too damn much for my own good.

Morning arrived far too soon. I'd thrashed about all night, waking and dozing. Now when I was usually at my best I felt as if I'd been pulled through the wringer and back again. This did not promise to be one of my better days. Leo was already in the kitchen when I came downstairs and when I said good-morning he immediately looked relieved.

'Nessa we didn't mean to shut you out, Raymond was only teasing and....'

'It's ok Leonard it's all in the past.'

'Then why are you calling me Leonard instead of Leo?'

'Oh I don't know, just a slip of the tongue, I didn't sleep well last night so let's just get on with it shall we?'

I could see he was confused by my behaviour but he didn't press the issue and without further conversation we began our regular routine. Breakfast for the first diners went as smoothly as could be expected under the circumstances but when Betty arrived, Leo suggested if I wanted to take the rest of the day off he'd ask her to stay. For once I agreed without arguing and went back to my bedroom, meaning to lie down for an hour and then go back and help. I crawled beneath the sheet in my underwear and the next thing I was aware of was a tapping at the door. A bit disoriented, thinking I was waking from my usual afternoon nap and Leo was bringing my tea, I said 'it's open come on in.' I had my back facing the door and when I heard it close, thinking Leo had left, I rolled over only to see Raymond looking down on me.

Oh it's you,' I spat out as I glared at him while pulling the sheet up to cover the fact I was clad only in my underwear, 'what are you doing here?'

'Aggie you are going to listen to me or else.'

'Or else what?' I challenged. 'May I remind you that you are in my room not yours.'

'Or else I'm going to take off my clothes and get in bed with you.'

'You wouldn't bloody well dare, I'd…' Any further protest was halted as he pulled his T shirt over his head and began to unbuckle his belt. 'Stop, stop that right now, I'll listen,' I said, knowing he was going to make good his threat.

'Is that a promise, I was only going to go as far as my underpants you know.'

' Yes, yes now will you let me get dressed first?'

'No I don't think so, I kind of like you this way, besides it's the only way I can be sure you won't stomp off.'

'I promise I'll listen to everything you have to say just let me put my clothes on.'

'Here then,' he said passing me my shirt and jeans.

'Aren't you even going to look away?' I asked,

'No I don't think so, as I told you I kind of like you this way' he replied.

I began to mutter making sure my words couldn't be understood and slipped into my shirt, quickly buttoning it. Then began the struggle of getting into my jeans beneath the sheet; all the while knowing he had a silly grin on that face I'd love to smack so hard he wouldn't know what hit him. It wouldn't have been a big deal to have dressed in front of him had it not been for his almighty attitude. Why does that man bring out such a strong stubborn streak in me? He can push all the right buttons and I always react. Damn him, damn him and damn me too I thought.

Sitting more or less comfortably on the side of the bed while Raymond sat in the arm chair I sipped my tea and steeled myself for what I thought was going to be a lecture. Wrong again.

'Nessie,' he began in a soft voice, 'I want you to stop fighting me.'

'Fighting you,' I repeated in a puzzled tone, 'I didn't know I was.'

'Well you are and you don't have to. I'm on your side in case you haven't figured it out.'

I was at a loss as to what to say, again things weren't going as I expected.

'Well,' I said 'I may have got the wrong end of the stick and guess I do owe you and Leo an apology. Neither of you are obligated to explain your actions to me so I shouldn't have expected you to do so.'

'Woman, woman, there you go again, pushing yourself outside when we want you on the inside with us. Of course you are due an explanation, you've given everything to help Leo and he knows it. He was close to tears last night when he thought we'd pushed you too far because you didn't know we were teasing. We may have met under unusual circumstances but that was then and this is now. We've become mates and we care about each other. Because of you Richard has his life back on track, Leo has renewed hope and

I've grown to care very much for a feisty lady and while I have nothing to base this on; I'm hoping in spite of everything she feels something for me too.'

Well that left absolutely nothing for me to say so that's exactly what I did say, nothing. Raymond stood up and left my room leaving me sitting on the bed wondering what had just happened. I think I remember him saying he cared for me and hoped I felt the same towards him. Was he daft? I couldn't get him out of my thoughts. Didn't he know, but then again how could he? I'd done everything in my power to prevent him from knowing how very much I cared.

I had to go down and speak to Leo. I wouldn't deliberately hurt him for anything in the world. For all his anger when I confessed my initial reason for intruding into his life I knew he was a gentle, compassionate man and it wasn't in his nature to wish harm on anyone. Unfortunately sometimes people with that degree of sensitivity are sorely taken advantage of. I accuse myself of doing that very thing at the beginning of our relationship but that was in the past and I hope I've moved on since.

Leo was nowhere to be seen in the house but when I glanced through the kitchen window I was pleasantly surprised to see him sitting in the garden. It was very seldom Leo could be seen taking a break but there he was, coffee cup in hand. As I exited the back door he looked up aware he was no longer alone, and it was then I saw the inner turmoil he felt reflected in his face. Realizing it was me his expression instantly turned to one of relief. I suspect Raymond had told him to wait for me to make the first move.

'Nessa,' he said, as he put his cup on the bench and walked towards me with arms extended.

I embraced him and whispered, 'Leo, please forgive me and my bad temper.'

'No Nessa, we went too far, even Raymond admitted men don't seem to know when to stop teasing but we didn't mean to upset you, honestly it wasn't intentional. We thought we were being funny and had no idea you'd take it the way you did.'

'I know Leo can we please forget it and start again?' He smiled and nodded his head looking as though he didn't trust his voice.

Then to break the tension I said, 'I think I'll get a coffee and join you, we don't get many opportunities to just sit and enjoy the garden do we?'

We talked about the upcoming bank meeting and Leo asked if I would wait till Raymond explained their plan as it would be Raymond approaching the bank on his behalf. Agreeing it would be best if the three of us were together we dropped the subject and began to discuss Leo's new girl, Anna. They had made plans to go to the pictures to-night with Richard and Carley. With the tourist season at an end Carley's position as a Whitby guide was finished for another year. She had returned to Raymond's hotel and taken up her old position with an added offer from Richard of training to be an assistant manager. He'd missed her while she'd worked in Whitby and knew he had to come up with something to entice her to remain with him. He was looking forward to proving to her how he'd changed and how much he'd always cared for her. Gossip reached him via the grapevine she'd gone out with a few lads in Whitby but the word was she didn't welcome any long term relationships or binding ties. He sincerely hoped he wasn't included in those feelings but was the reason for them.

Finally the cool evening air drove us inside to think about dinner. There were leftovers and I suggested we have those as he would probably be stopping to have something to eat with Anna after the pictures. Leo wolfed down a few mouthfuls then excusing himself, said he needed time to shower and left the table and the rest of the meal to me. He'd been out with Anna a few times and I got the impression he thought she was pretty special. Her Father definitely thought she was special from what Leo said as he told me of their conversations whenever he arrived to pick up Anna from the pub. As if it weren't enough to face her Father, he also had to run the gamut of the older regulars who felt it was their loyal duty to offer dire warnings should any harm come to their favourite lass. Leo said by the time the two of them reached his car he was in a sweat.

Clearing away the few dishes and making sure everything was ready for breakfast, I thought that as I had the evening to myself I'd change to pyjamas and robe and begin the new novel I'd purchased, in what now seemed ages ago. It was about a woman close to my age, and the trials and tribulations she experienced as she went about the difficult task of creating a new life for herself after the sudden death of her husband.

Chapter Thirteen

The evenings were coming on dark earlier as the days passed and it was a reminder that I still had a house of my own to take care of. I'd been away over six months and didn't have any plans in the offing of a permanent return. As I began to think about the future I had to admit I had my own issues to deal with. I decided that as soon as the business concerning Leo's bank financing was cleared up I'd return to my own home and make some serious decisions. After all this was never meant to be a permanent arrangement. It was my way of making retribution and when I felt it had been done, I needed to get on with my life, just like the woman in my novel. The more and more I thought about it the more miserable I felt. The novel lay in my lap, turned to the same page as when I'd last opened it. Losing all track of time it was only the chimes of the mantle clock that brought me back to the present. They were a reminder of how long I'd been engrossed in contemplating the consequences if I left this life I thrived on and even now, the regret I would feel. Yes I still had a bit of a temper, and yes I still got bent out of shape when I let something bother me when I shouldn't but I was improving, even I could see that. What was the difference after all this time: how was my life different and who was in my life now that hadn't been there before? It was only last week I pulled on those tight trousers of the pant suit I'd worn when I started my adventures, and found they were now too big. As that was my best dress up outfit I'd gone to an M&S sale to purchase a replacement and found I'd dropped a full size with room to spare. What accounts for this? What about new friends, Betty, Leo, Richard, Raymond. Then there was Pat the town butcher who always gave the kiddies a piece of cooked sausage, Neil the bus driver who drives too fast, Edwin the baker who maintained a dozen still added up to thirteen in his shop. All new, all part of my life as it is now. This is going to be much harder than I could ever have imagined. I decided to go to bed. Reading wasn't conducive to my current state of mind so whatever I did read would have to be reread next time I picked up the book. I turned out the lights and had started up the stairs to my room when the phone rang. It was Leo.

'Nessa, I need your help, can you phone Anna's Dad and tell him she's staying at Raymond's hotel because I've had car trouble?'

'Leo, are you bloody mad it's almost midnight.'

'I know but he'll just be closing up the pub and will still be there.'

'Leo is it asking too much to ask why you aren't taking her home; like I don't already know from the sound of your voice.'

'Sorry Nessa, I've had too much to drink and can't drive.'

'Bloody hell where are you and why can't you just get a cab?'

'We're still outside the club Claret. Anna had too much to drink and she's sick too so I can't take her home in that condition or her Dad will kill me.'

'Alright you daft bugger I'll call him and tell him you've had car trouble and reassure him his daughter's virtue is safe. 'Where's Richard and Carley?'

'They only had one drink after the pictures and then left for the hotel. Wait Nessa, I've got a call coming in from Raymond.'

'Call me back Leo,' I said, and hung up.

A few minutes later the phone rang. This time it was Raymond.

'Go to bed Aggie, everything is taken care of. Richard told me Leo didn't want to leave when he and Carley did and suspecting something like this might happen, warned me I might be getting getting a call to rescue them. After speaking to Leo I called Anna's Dad and told him she'll be well taken care of. Right now I'm on my way to pick up our two tear-a-ways.'

'Raymond I'm going to stay up till you get here.'

'Alright Nessie that's good to hear, see you in a bit.'

About an hour later, Raymond escorted a very sheepish Leo to his bedroom and then returned to the lounge.

'Anna's asleep in the car, she certainly won't be sick again to-night, in fact she may never be sick again ever.'

'That bad was it?' I asked.

'Oh you know, young couples with raging hormones trying to get up the courage to tell each other how they feel. When they realized one drink made them feel relaxed and talkative, it was a foregone conclusion another would be even better.'

'Do you want coffee Raymond?'

'May as well, there won't be much sleep to-night anyway'

I made instant coffee and we sat sipping at the kitchen table.

'Have you and Leo made up?' he asked.

'Of course Raymond, how could we not? I should tell you he didn't go into any details regarding your plans for the bank, saying he thought it preferable if we three were together and I agreed.'

'Nessie I'm so sorry about all that.'

'For what?' I asked, unsure of what he was apologizing for.

'Too much teasing at the wrong time and then too heavy handed trying to make you see the error of your ways.'

Ah, now I knew where he was coming from. 'Well Raymond, I must admit you certainly got my attention when you began your strip tease but other than that, I do admit to being put out because I thought you and Leo hadn't included me in your plans.'

'Does that matter to you Nessie, if you're not included in our plans?'

'Of course it does, do you think I care nothing for Leo and his problems?' I asked.

'Oh I know you care for Leo,' he responded, 'I guess I was just fishing for conformation that you might care for me too and would be hurt if you weren't included in my plans as well as Leo's.'

'Raymond what do you want me to say?'

'What do you think I want you to say? If you want me to spell it out for you I will.'

'Sorry Raymond, but from my point of view it doesn't seem a particularly good idea to let you know just what my feelings are at the moment.'

'Not a lot of trust going on is there?'

'No not right now, but maybe it's time to say goodnight anyway. I fear I'm Cinderella and on the verge of soon being found sitting amongst the cinders again.'

Next mornning Leo looked surprisingly well considering his condition the night before.

'Nessa I'm so sorry about last night,' he began.

'Leo we all pull these stunts when we're growing up, the thing is to learn from them and not repeat them.'

With a look of relief that I wouldn't be delivering a chastising lecture, he enveloped me in his arms and kissed me on the cheek before hugging me saying, 'my Mama Nessa you're the best.'

Chapter Fourteen

As the days passed Leo and I continued to work in harmony in spite of the ever present money worries. Anna sometimes came to dinner now and Leo would try to outdo himself each time as he summoned all his skills to prepare a meal that would impress her. He was truly besotted and she obviously felt the same. We asked her parents, Ve and Charles, for dinner one night and it went surprisingly smooth. Raymond came too and in spite of our varied natures and life interests, we got along well and found enough common ground to want to repeat the experience. Charles much in favour of this, initiated the next get together by inviting us to his pub for a quiz night. Ve was a wonderful hostess and served delicious sandwiches and bits to nibble on at half time. To our surprise Raymond and I came first in the quiz, winning a bottle of white wine and a pretty house plant. Smiling ever so smugly at our younger competitors I think we enjoyed the gloating more than the winning. Richard promptly stood, and directing his words to the room at large said he thought his Dad was reasonably smart but not that smart. Then to show his support for a fellow quizzer, Leo followed up with his own proclamation saying he didn't realize his under paid help had a brain too. All amid loud applause which encouraged more banter until Leo, finally observing my personal sign language indicating his life was in danger, very shortly sat down. At last with boasts and promises made as to who would win next, along with not so subtle aspersions cast on the intelligence of family, friends, and past generations, we headed homeward. Leo, siezing the opportunity to sneak away with Anna for a private moment, lagged behind while Richard and Carley headed for their mutual domain at the hotel. That left Raymond and I to walk back to Leo's house alone. Raymond took my hand as we fell into step. I had really fallen for this man and knew it. He didn't seem to want to get rid of me but I didn't know why. It was the Peacock and Wood Pigeon story. It bothered me because I was afraid of being hurt again and knew instinctively Raymond's feelings and behaviour towards me would have an enormous impact on the rest of my life. There, I'd finally admitted it to myself.

I was as besotted with Raymond as Leo was with Anna, maybe more so and I was old enough to know better but obviously didn't. Reaching the front door Raymond said, 'Aggie, Leo offered me a room for the night to save me the trip back to the hotel. My appointment with the manager is to-morrow afternoon and I want to spend some time going over the final figures and statements before then.'

'Oh he never mentioned it, did he say which room?'

'No but he said he'd leave a key with my name on it.'

'No problem then, I'll check after I put the kettle on, you do want tea don't you?'

'Yup that's fine and a piece of toast if you don't mind.'

'Toast, why toast?'

'Don't know, just like a piece of toast after a night out' he answered.

Pushing the bread down in the toaster I thought there was so much more to learn about this man and I was eagerly looking forward to it all. Tea made and waiting for it to brew, I went to the front desk to pick up Raymond's key. There it was, sporting a tag with his name spelled out in big black marking pen letters. Leo, dear romantic soul that he was, put Raymond in room ten with a connecting door to room twelve, my room. Bless that lovely boy, to-morrow I'm going to kill him after I explain some of the facts of life to him. Ungrateful whelp that he is; does he think I'm made of stone or does he just think I'm past it?

Raymond and I finished our tea and toast and finally went upstairs, he to his room and me to mine. He gave me a quick kiss and hug at the door and we said good-night. I don't know if I was pleased or annoyed but I was too tired to give it much thought.

By the time I went downstairs in the morning the kitchen was in full swing. Too much liquor didn't stop Leo from his duties the morning after, no matter how he felt.

'Good morning my little match maker,' I said to him in greeting.

'Whatever do you mean Nessa?'

I heard the grin in his voice without ever having to see his face.

'Didn't work you know. Raymond and I are far too mature to take advantage of some besotted lad that wants the world to fall in love just because he did.' Leo turned to face me and I was quite taken aback to see the shocked look on his face as though I'd discovered what he thought was a well hidden secret.

He actually blushed as he said, 'didn't mean any harm Nessa.'

'And certainly no harm done Leo,' I replied, in a bit of a cheeky tone. Again from the look on his face I saw this was an even more sensitive subject than I'd guessed so said no more and we got on with the business of serving our guests. Raymond came downstairs as serving was in full swing and going through, sat at the kitchen table to have his breakfast all the while chatting to Leo of the upcoming meeting. As I poured coffee for him I felt his arm go about my middle pulling me close, gently squeezing my waist just to let me know he knew I was there too. It's amazing how a touch from the right person changes your mood and outlook.

Raymond's appointment at the bank was at 2 o'clock. This time he went alone leaving Leo and I to wait together at home. Sitting side by side on the sofa we found we had little to say to one another, only occasionally attempting to make idle conversation. Finally we gave up all attempts. Shoulders hunched as though to protect ourselves from the final coup de grace, we remained silent with our thoughts. How much kinder if the appointment had been during the morning hours when we would have had our bodies and minds occupied with the housekeeping chores. As it was we'd been wringing our hands this past hour and had no idea how much longer we would have to wait to hear the outcome. It seemed a good time to inform Leo of my upcoming plans and the need to be away a day or two.

'Leo I'm going to have to go back and check on my house again. I don't want you to think I'm bailing out on you whatever the banks decision and that's why I'm telling you now. No matter what happens I'll be here for you, to help in whatever way I can.'

Putting his arm about my shoulders and looking straight into my eyes Leo said, 'Nessa I didn't know how much I needed you in my life until you arrived.'

That did it, too much love and caring for two people who had felt very little of either in their lonely lives. I pulled him towards me and as we wrapped our arms about each other, the two of us wept at our good fortune to have met when we did. Leo finally felt a mother's love and I the renewed love of a son again. Amidst the joy of our unexpected reunion we also saw the humour in the situation and began to laugh at ourselves, and none too soon. At this point Raymond returned and with our hearts bursting with expectation, we waited. Neither of us had the courage to ask the outcome of the meeting till he spoke .

'Well aren't you two a fine looking pair? Tears in your eyes, laughter on your lips and worry wrinkling your brows, what a confused greeting for a man that's gone to the wall for you. Shall I release you from the suspense?'

'Raymond,' I said, with a menacing threat to my voice.

'Oh calm down my feisty woman, I shan't keep either of you waiting.'

Glancing at Leo, Raymond saw he was in a state of near agony and immediately reassured him. 'It's going to be alright Leo, we've got an extension.' Leo's sigh of relief could have been heard down the street.

'Raymond please,' he said, 'tell us what we've got to work with.'

'Well as of to-day we have a guarantee of a six month extension on the mortgage providing we can come up with the interest and a bit more to show our good faith.'

Leo looked to me, 'can we manage that Nessa?'

'I think so, we've been putting a bit aside for emergencies and can use that towards the extra payment they expect. If we ask Betty to come on a regular basis we can operate with almost a full house.'

I noticed Raymond's brow had become slightly furrowed, as though he had another message to relay and that it just might tarnish the shine of Leo's relief. Why wasn't he as pleased as Leo and I at the good news?

'Raymond, why don't you look as happy as we feel, what are you holding back?' There was an overshadowing chill in the previously joyous feeling in the room. It was confusing, how could such good news herald the foreboding of bad news too? Looking at both of us he answered in a sombre toned voice,

'It is good news we've obtained a bit more time to plan but you must both understand this is only a stop gap. This is not going to make everything better. Leo, I am going to speak to you as a father. I have many years of experience behind me of running and owning a business. You, my lad, are not cut out for business. Your heart is in the kitchen and a B&B will never let you realize your dreams to become all you were meant to be. My best advice to you is use the six months to sell the house and bank any monies realized for the day you will want to buy your own restaurant.'

'Aggie, I know you'd do anything for Leo and as much as I admire you for that I hope you'll see the truth in my reasoning and advice and won't encourage him to hang on just for the sake of not giving in. Sometimes people feel they've failed if they switch dreams in mid- stream, whereas in fact they've actually grasped the true dream.'

Damn, but that Raymond did have a good mind and I've always found that very attractive in a man. As for Leo, after absorbing the initial shock of Raymond's announcements, he spoke up.

'I think I know what you mean Raymond I guess I didn't want to deal with what happened with Devon and Sharon so made up my mind I'd show them I didn't need them. That part is true I didn't need them or anyone like them. What I've needed for so long is someone to tell me the truth as they see it and someone to back me up whatever my decision. How come I'm so fortunate to now have both? Thank-you Raymond, I know you're right and guess at the back of my mind have known it for a while but just needed a good friend to risk saying it to my face. You're that good friend and I owe you big time.'

'You owe me nothing Leo, you're a talented lad and given the right opportunity you'll make a name for yourself. If I have been or can ever be of any help along the way, then it will be my privilege to do all within my power to make it happen.'

Both of them looked to me. 'Well what do you two thugs expect me to say? I'm with you all the way and you know it.'

Chapter Fifteen

Leo decided to put the house up for sale and as if to bestow a blessing on his decision, he met the perfect person to list with. A young fellow was having lunch at Ve and Charles' pub while Leo waited for Anna to finish work and eventually the two men began to chat, with the conversation turning to what each did for a living. Though a novice estate agent the young man could forsee the sale of Leo's house at an excellent price and told him so. To his credit as a up and coming salesman, when their conversation concluded, he was overjoyed to learn Leo would consider him for the job. Next day we all met and the eager entrepreneur was determined to show his stuff. He set about convincing us that with a minimal amount of cosmetic improvements, the house would be the proverbial goldmine. Totally forthcoming of his intent to succeed he wasted no time admitting there was much profit to be had, not only for Leo and the new owner, but for himself as well. As primary agent, he would reap the maximum commission and with this incentive he entered into the agreement with great enthusiasm. The present market was on the rise so not wanting to hesitate when the timing was so auspicious he suggested Leo offer it immediately. Also at his suggestion, Leo agreed to describe the house as an established business. This justified a much higher asking price than any of us thought reasonable for a quick sale but in spite of our doubts, we were assured that within a few days it would be on every estate agent's most preferred list. The decision to sell and the young agent's honesty infused us with new life, at last we felt we were finally moving forward and not just breaking even. For my part, I arranged with Betty to cover my work for a few days enabling me to return to my own house and deal with some personal matters I'd been putting off for some time. It would be an imposition to impose on Maureen any longer and I valued her friendship far too much to let that happen. I kept the main reason for visiting my property secret but reasoned if Leo could sell his house then I could sell mine, it meant nothing to me now. My life and home was here with my family of friends and I wanted to be on hand to see that Leo's house was ready at a moments notice for viewings. Once I acknowledged this there was no need for delay in putting my plan in motion. The feeling of happiness I now felt gave me the added reassurance it was meant to be and, as with Leo's decision to accept a revised plan enabling him to move on, I too felt I was moving on and not just keeping up. With an optimistic outlook, only slightly tinged by a somewhat disturbing but fleeting sense of urgency which I was determined not to let spoil my new adventure, I began. After packing a few things and making a list of what needed doing I was ready to leave. If I left Saturday morning I'd have enough time to take care of everything and return Monday afternoon, ready to resume my duties on Tuesday morning for the breakfast start. For now and over the next few days, it would be a concentrated effort to make Leo's house shine as never before. I had no doubt his estate agent would have the ball rolling immediately, the anticipation of a large commission would be his greatest inspiration. Not only was he filled with the boundless energy of youth but he was eager and greedy for success, lucky Leo.

Raymond joined us for dinner on Friday and when Leo told him I was off in the morning he offered to drive me, saving a tiresome bus journey The offer was too good to refuse, lately we'd both been too busy to think of ourselves and any opportunities to be together were not only minimal but short at the best of times. I missed him more than just a bit, too damn much if truth be told, and all I could wish for was that he missed me too

Hoping to impress Raymond more than usual, Leo made a roast dinner that would tempt a vegetarian. Truly he had the makings of a marvellous chef. Richard had confided that whenever Anna was busy, Leo was at the Chapel and Chimes begging Chef Aidan to let him help. Aidan had informed his boss of these offers of free kitchen help and this was what had prompted Raymond to speak when he did. In making Leo aware of where his true talents lay, he had done him a true favour before the young man invested any more time and money in the B & B.

After dinner Leo was off to see Anna. She was working to-night at her parent's pub but Leo didn't mind as she'd be finished by nine and they'd have the rest of the evening to themselves. Usually they spent weekends with Richard and Carley but when Leo explained to them he'd put the house up for sale, they understood his time would be limited for a while, wanting to spend every free minute with Anna. Charles and Ve approved of Leo and considered

Richard and Carley suitable friends for their daughter. They were old fashioned in their thinking in spite of allowing their daughter to work in the pub. However they tolerated no disrespect towards their only offspring. One look from Charles and even the pub regulars cleaned up their language. A more diplomatic Ve, while fully supporting her husband, did her bit and kept them coming back with her sumptuous cooking and occasional understanding nods that said, 'don't take offence, you know how men are when it comes to their daughters.' But if truth be told she was every bit as protective as Charles and would have personally thrashed any man showing disrespect towards her beloved child. Raymond left shortly after Leo, saying he had a few hotel matters to deal with before it got too late and would be back to pick me up about eight next morning. It had been a busy day and I didn't object to having the rest of the evening to myself for last minute thinking. I had a quick shower and was snuggled down in bed with a good book before ten. Just what I needed I thought drowsily, and as if to prove my point, in the morning I couldn't recall a single word I'd read. Raymond arrived shortly before eight and after a quick coffee we pulled out of the driveway. The weather showed promised of a pleasant drive and I was content to look at the passing scenery.

It was Raymond who broke the silence, 'you're unusually quiet, is everything alright?'

'I've decided to sell my house and move closer to Leo so if he needs my help I'm available.'

Raymond said nothing for a moment then, 'it's obvious that you and Leo have developed a close relationship, I noticed he's taken to calling you Nessa, his own pet name for you. I think I understand Leo and as close as he is to a happy future with Anna I think he still feels the lack of a mother in his life. He told me a little of his childhood and believe me, it was a pretty dismal time for any child let alone a sensitive boy like Leo. Unlike his neighbour Betty's grandchild, there was no loving grandmother waiting on the side lines for him, in fact there was no one at all at any time in his young life. I'm sure that lack of love and caring as a youngster has made him easy prey to people like Devon and Sharon. Nevertheless, I don't want to see you hurt and as long as you're aware he's a young man with his foot at the door, you won't be when he doesn't need you quite as much in the future as he does now.'

'Yes I do know that Raymond but I thank-you for your honesty and your caring too.'

Taking his hand from the steering wheel he reached over and took my hand in his and squeezing gently said, 'you really are a lovely feisty woman and I find you very easy to care about whether you know it or not.' His words sent a soft glow through me and again I was content to say nothing. This man is having a strange effect on me I wonder what it is about him that can bring out the best in me and if I'm honest, the worst too?

Traffic on the motor way was light and we reached my little house in good time. Once through the front door it took only a few moments to unload the boot and after switching on the heat, I immediately got on the phone and managed to arrange an appointment with an agent for to-morrow morning.

Between the two of us we had everything dusted and tidy by late afternoon and with the last of the garden flowers creating their magic, the lounge took on that cosy lived in look again. While we were admiring our handy-work, Maureen came over to invite us for tea and cake. It was the perfect time for a much needed break and we were happy to accept. Raymond quickly finished his tea and excused himself saying he wanted to mow the lawns for the final time this year, telling Maureen he'd cut hers too. This was an excellent opportunity for me to not only settle my accounts with Maureen but let her know how much she meant to me. Her brown eyes shone as they filled with tears and I knew she had been dreading the time we would be parted. It was obvious she needed reassurance that our friendship was not dependent upon being next door neighbours but went much deeper than that. I began to speak from my heart and soon saw her face brighten as I reminded her we had shared so much, far too much to ever be discarded by a change of address. Returning to my house I thought how strange that we can feel so close to a person but forget to tell them how much they mean to us, assuming they would surely know. Talking to Maureen reminded me it's not always enough to feel affection but sometimes necessary to hear words of love as well. Face to face, to tell another how important they are to us and the deep impact their friendship has made in our lives.

Later Raymond and I sat in the garden, hands touching, melding body and mind as we sipped a final glass of wine and inhaled the scent of the fresh cut grass. The damp chill of autumn air foretold the end of days when it would be not be warm enough to sit outside and experience this colourful change of season. We both loved this time of year so were loath to end a precious and almost sacred awareness of the moment. Shrouding ourselves in car robes we remained where we were till it became too dark to see each other and finally were driven inside by hunger. Nothing planned for dinner, Raymond suggested he drive to the local chippy and get us a takeaway. While he was gone I set the table and buttered some bread. Hearing a noise at the door and thinking it was Raymond I was surprised to see Maureen holding a basket.

'I know you planned to pop out for breakfast but after all your rushing about to-day I thought you might appreciate a lie in and then have breakfast when you were ready. Oh and by the way, I've put in a bit of that cake you liked, it's enough to do you for your desert to-night'.

Thanking her again for her generosity I was reminded once more of what a truly good friend she was. The basket contained everything we needed for a good breakfast even sauces and marmalade. When I showed Raymond, he suggested once we were home again and settled we invite her for a weekend and take her to his restaurant. I was thrilled with the idea and told him I would so look forward to treating her for a change. I also thought she and Betty might enjoy each other's company and Raymond agreed saying we would invite them at the same time, giving them a chance to discover what they had in common.

What a busy but lovely day it had been. Our fish and chip dinner was just nothing short of perfection, but some of that could have been due to the fact we were both ravenous in spite of Maureen's tea break. Even the slice of bread and butter tasted as though I was savouring it for the first time. I couldn't explain it to myself let alone Raymond so I said nothing, thinking I was in one of my fanciful moods. Raymond finished his cake and coffee as I went for a shower. Then remembering I hadn't done so earlier, I got a bath towel and face cloth and laid it on Raymond's bed. With doors and windows open all day the house was well aired but now had cooled considerably so I closed the window of his room and did the same in mine.

Although the water was barely warm the shower was reviving and refreshing and I returned to the lounge in my pyjamas and dressing gown to towel dry my hair. I'd forgotten the blow dryer and wasn't going to bother Maureen for the use of hers.

'Well don't you look as fresh as a daisy?' Raymond commented.

'Behave yourself,' I retorted, ' or I won't heat any more water and you'll have to have a cold shower.'

'Hmm, sounds interesting but is there going to be a need for that?' I knew instantly I'd said the wrong thing and given him an opening to be suggestive.

'Don't you dare say anything more Raymond or I won't be responsible for my actions,' I warned him.

'Oh sounds even better,' he said, ducking the swiftly thrown cushion.

While Raymond was in the shower I washed the few dishes and set the table for breakfast. I asked at the bathroom door if he had everything he needed and receiving an affirmative reply, went to the lounge and lit a small fire hoping to dispel the chill in the room. I'd left the house wide open to air throughout the day but left it far too late into the evening because I hadn't wanted to interrupt our last moments in the garden, now the whole house had somehow taken on a feeling of emptiness, even neglect. For whatever reason it made me feel lonely, something I'd not felt in a long time and with plans to spend the evening on my 'to do' list and with hair still damp, I was feeling the need for a bit of warmth. There'd be plenty of time before the estate agent arrived in the morning to clean out the grate so I splurged on a bit of wood with golden pitch oozing down the rough, crusted, bark. That would see us through the evening and maybe take the edge off the chill in the morning too.

Why am I always thinking about time? Worrying about time to clean the grate, how ridiculous! What possible difference could it make if I do or don't remove the ashes from the grate? It's perfectly natural for a grate to have ashes and that certainly won't be the deciding factor of whether a buyer decides to buy or not. My time here is short and I don't want to overlook anything of importance so maybe I should take to spending that limited commodity on what is of real importance in the overall scheme of things. Lately, in one of my many moments of reflection, I've become very conscious of the briefness of a lifetime. Is that why I'm so incredibly happy now? Is it because I'm learning to live in the moment rather than anticipating what lies ahead and trying to predict the unpredictable? Have I finally understood, at a soul level, there aren't any guarantees in life? Maybe I'm experiencing another of my fanciful moods but if so in the end it doesn't matter, it just is and so am I.

Knotting the sash to his dressing gown Raymond came into the lounge and as he sat next to me on the sofa I offered him the list to double check. Expressing my concerns of missing something he reassured me.

'Don't worry about the minor things Nessie. So much can be done by email. Million pound deals are finalized without the parties ever meeting.'

'Sorry Raymond I know my concerns must seem so trivial to you. I guess in some ways I'm still back in the dark ages. My business dealings had to be done without help or advice from anyone I could trust so I guess that's why I'm a little fanatical about crossing T's and dotting I's in person.

'You don't have to apologize for that Nessie. I think you've taken care of yourself and others remarkably well. It's a lot more than many others could say under the same circumstances. If selling your lovely little cottage means you want to do it in a way that has proven successful in the past, there are none that have the right to deny you, but I don't want you to worry. You're not alone this time and I can only hope you consider me worthy of your trust.'

Everything about this man boosts my confidence and validates me. Why hadn't he happened earlier in my life? What a very different life it would have been. What talent does he possess that gives him the ability to peer into my soul? He touches the very heart of me on so many levels and in so many ways that I don't understand. He frightens me and he comforts me, he makes me laugh till tears come to my eyes and he infuriates me to a point just short of murder. If God in heaven loves this difficult child of his, I pray he never lets that lovely man know how truly besotted with him I am, for surely I would be lost forever in the love of it all.

We both sat and read till ten thirty. Closing my book I told Raymond I was going to bed. Asking him to be sure the doors were locked and the lights out, I leaned over his shoulder and kissed him on the cheek. Reaching up to my face his hand lingered in a caress that seemed to burn its imprint onto my skin. For fear he'd see the flush on my cheeks I immediately turned and walking towards my room said, 'see you at breakfast,' then quickly shut my door to block out hearing any reply.

I lay in bed for what seemed ages. I was tired but couldn't close my eyes, I felt safe but threatened. Finally I managed to doze off into a fitful half sleep, dreamlike yet somehow still awake. Snippets of dreams would bring me back to full awareness and then I would doze off again and repeat the process. Encroaching on my dreams I thought I heard the sound of wind brushing a branch against the window. It brought me back to full wakefulness and I sat up, immediately realizing the sound was not part of my dream, it was real and it was a tapping at my door.

'Nessie, are you awake?'

'The door's not locked Raymond,' I answered.

The soft glow from the hall lamp outlined his shape as the door swung wide. He didn't move or say anything for a moment then slowly entered the room to stand beside the night table. Looking down upon me I heard him say ever so softly, 'Nessie I want to sleep with you.'

I made no reply but moved over to the far side of the bed and turned back the covers in invitation. He remained where he was for what seemed like forever, then removing his dressing gown, slid between the crisp sheets to enclose me in his arms.

We spent ourselves not like the frantic love starved youth, but by instinctively knowing in the giving we were receiving. Each caress was a new experience, each touch a new discovery. It was what youth should have been, but could never be without the gifts of time and maturity. The night was moving towards dawn before we closed our eyes and slept the drugged sleep of passion. Peaceful, exhausted, once again having validated life itself.

Waking first, I rose and went to the kitchen to heat water for our showers and make some coffee. I didn't know how to explain last night but somehow now that it had happened I was amazed I hadn't realized it was inevitable. Leo had known, so how many others knew? Even Maureen had anticipated we wouldn't want an early morning and had supplied a breakfast for two layabouts. Oh hell, had Raymond known all along and am I the only ignorant innocent? And why now do I subject myself to all these doubts? I'd just spent the night in a state of bliss that I didn't know existed? Was it a leftover from that early belief system that had been hammered into my mind from childhood that if it's sunny to-day, surely it will rain to-morrow? No glimmer of happiness without a shadow of gloom hovering near. There's never enough to go around. Don't expect happiness because you don't deserve it and won't get it. I thought I had exorcised that demon but obviously when I reached this state of happiness it was right back, rearing its ugly head to remind me that it won't last. Damn, damn and another damn. I won't let it destroy what I've had, even if I never experience it again, nothing can wipe it from my memory. Somehow in my heart of hearts I knew this loving thing was always there, but I hadn't known how to reach it. Raymond had shown me the way and no matter what else happens, for that alone I can never repay him for what he's given me.

Showered and with cups of coffee in hand I returned to the bedroom. Raymond was still asleep so placing the cups on the bed side table I took the opportunity to gaze on his features in secret, denying him the awareness of being observed. I wanted to reach out and caress his face, tracing my fingers from his brow to chin, exploring each curve and contour till they became imprinted on my mind and, if I was blinded to-morrow I could still caress his profile. Lost in reverie it was he who caught me off guard saying, 'did you bring me one too?' He had been aware of my presence but had not interrupted my scrutiny of his features.

'How long have you been awake,' I asked, 'oh just long enough to smell the coffee and wonder where mine was' he answered.

'Right here,' I said, reaching for his cup. But before I could do so he pulled me towards him.

'So my Nessie, are you as happy as I am?'

'Do you mean that Raymond or is this just something to say to get past the awkward bit?'

I don't know why I said this and it infuriated him.

'What the hell is the matter with you woman? I've just spent the most wonderful night of my life and you think I'm making small talk.'

'No, no Raymond, I didn't mean to say that, I didn't want to say it because I know it's not true. I don't think you're making small talk but I can't believe you felt what I did.'

'Can't you now, well just let me show you once again to prove what I say is true.' Thus said our coffee remained untouched and breakfast was delayed a little longer.

The estate agent was due to arrive and we still had the bed to make.

'This is not funny Raymond the whole neighbourhood will know what we've been up to.'

'And your point is?' he asked.

'Oh do be quiet and fluff the pillows,' I said, not having any point to make.

The agent was on time and after looking over the house and garden suggested I list at a price a bit higher than I would have thought reasonable. She explained the market was still experiencing an upward trend so it wouldn't hurt to try and I could always drop my price later if necessary. Raymond agreed with her so I happily signed the listing for a three month period.

After the agent left Raymond phoned Leo and said due to such short notice we couldn't get an estate agent to view the house till to-morrow so would not be able to return till Tuesday evening. Could Betty cover my shift for one more day? With Leo's reassurances they could manage, he then got on the phone to Richard and gave him the same story. Richard being a bit older and more experienced than Leo didn't buy into his Father's explanation and suggested, tongue in cheek maybe this was just what his Dad needed, a change of scene and a few days off his feet. As much as Raymond tried to convince me his son had swallowed the story, I knew it hadn't happened that way and told him so.

He looked at me and said, 'do you mind so very much Nessie? Is what they know or think they know, important to you?'

'No Raymond,' I replied, 'but what is important is what you know and think.'

'Are you not aware of that by now, is my mind and body obsessed by a crazed daft woman, does she need more convincing?' So saying he wrapped his arms about me, drew me close and proceeded to convince me all over again.

The rest of the day and into the next we spent reading, relaxing, cooking dinner and enjoying our own company. Tuesday herald the end to what had become an unexpected lover's tryst. We went out for breakfast then walked beside the stream bank till rain drove us back to the house for a last tidy up. I looked at my soon to be sold home fondly, but with no regrets at saying good-bye, it was time to move on.

We started back to the hotel in the late afternoon. The return trip was uneventful and our only stop was to pick up a

Chinese takeaway. Raymond had phoned Richard asking who would be home for dinner and ordered enough food for all. Having a ready prepared meal would give us the opportunity to sit down and discuss our plans with everyone at the same time. I was already looking forward to their reactions and even the inevitable cheeky innuendos that would come from Richard couldn't faze me now. To be together again was all that mattered no matter how much teasing was to be endured. It seemed we had melded into an extended family group and teasing was only just that, a playful way of declaring a certain accepted familiarity and fondness for one another. It was a new experience for me, this teasing thing, and I was learning it was possible to enter into the exchange of banter without the maliciousness I had formerly associated with it.

Chapter Sixteen

Though the last warmth of autumn was now past and chill night air reminded us of bitterly cold winter winds yet to come, it did nothing to dispel the memories of the sweetness of the days and nights Raymond and I had spent together. And as if to place a seal of approval on our new relationship, two weeks after we returned from our tryst, I received a call from the estate agent advising me of an offer on my house. It was just under the listed price and I didn't hesitate to accept. In less than two months I would hand over the keys and for the first time in a long time have extra money to spend for Christmas gifts. Nearer to the closing date Raymond and I would go back and clear out my personal effects but other than that I was leaving the furniture for the new owners, a young couple who were thankful for any extra bits. In gratitude for her unstinting help, I told Maureen whatever she fancied was hers for the asking and she was delighted to have some lamps she had long admired. Raymond insisted I notify my family of my upcoming move to Yorkshire and give them the hotel address as my permanent residence. As much as I didn't want to, I knew he was right so I got off a short note to the eldest telling him to forward the news to his siblings. Although it was never my intention to seek revenge I must admit it did cross my mind it would be priceless just to see the looks on their faces when they realized my house was now permanently out of their reach. Nor had I anticipated the relief I would experience when I finally realized that particular door of my life was at last closed, and within the time it took for my heart to beat, a new door had already opened.

At the beginning of November just before the sale of my house was to be finalized, Leo received a great offer on his B&B and would be handing over the keys early in January. I couldn't help but think that ever since Raymond and I had declared our feelings for each other life seemed to be looking up for everyone. Then it flashed through my mind this would be a year to remember. How odd to think that I mused but then, I'd had so many unexplainable thoughts lately that I'd made a point of not expending too much time looking for hidden meanings. I was happy, incredibly happy, so very happy in fact that I'd learned to dismiss many things that couldn't be explained. I'd learned to let my mind appreciate how it was not only amazing but heart-warming as well that in such a short space of time we had become as close as any blood related family. Surprisingly for me was that what affected one affected all, so much so that as a bonded family we felt our happiness was forever increasing while our sorrows were diminishing.

One Sunday, after enjoying a family dinner cooked by Carley and Anna, Raymond and I were on the verge of returning to our suite when Richard mentioned he and Leo wanted our opinion on something they had in mind. We followed the boys into the study and they immediately got down to business and proceeded to tell Raymond and me of their plans for the future. They had certainly done their homework and we told them so. With our approval at this point they then informed us of their decision to enter into a partnership. As far as they were concerned this was a prime factor towards the success of their enterprise. After paying off his debts, Leo would invest the small profit from the sale of his house at the highest interest rate possible carrying the minimal degree of risk. He would work part time for Raymond at the hotel and would also be at Chef Aidan's disposal, endeavouring to gain further experience at the Chapel and Chimes restaurant. Some time ago Chef Aidan had convinced Raymond that Leo should be on the pay roll as he did the work of a full time employee even while working as an unpaid volunteer. Richard's contribution would entail taking further business management courses while remaining assistant manager for his Father. The two were convinced that with Leo in the kitchen and Richard at the desk they could build a business capable of expanding to a chain of hotels. I was totally impressed with their ambitions and commitments. To my mind their combined talents were a recipe for success, all in all a very attractive package, however I remained quiet. I wanted to say something encouraging but as the one with the least experience and insight into these matters, didn't think it my place to offer an opinion.

Raymond listened intently then looking to me said he thought we should discuss it privately in a little more detail before we offered our opinions. I could hardly believe my ears; he was going to discuss this with me first? They all smiled and seemed to think this was right and proper and the way it should be. Leo beamed from ear to ear as Richard said, 'thanks Dad and Aggie, you know we value your advice,' and all nodded their heads in agreement.

When Raymond and I were behind closed doors I made him look directly at me. 'Raymond did you mean that or was it just a delay tactic?'

'Oh my God woman, are we to go through this again, how many times must I tell you…'

'I know, I know, I'm sorry Raymond, forget I said anything,' I pleaded, as I leaned my head on his chest.

'No, this time you must pay a penalty,' he said, with a lecherous grin, so what else could I do but convince him I was frightened as I hugged him closer.

A few days later Raymond reminded me I still had a few personal items to collect from my house and it would be a good idea to gather them up before bad weather set in. There was just over a week till I would turn over the keys so I agreed we'd drive down, pack the last bits and return home as soon as possible to help ready the hotel for the Christmas season. I resented having to be away just now and knew I should have taken care of this earlier but the days had passed so quickly. My life had become filled with people and I was just so incredibly happy that somehow material things had faded into the background. Maybe this was also a contributing factor as to why I had become preoccupied with thoughts of grandchildren. When I spoke to Raymond about this he reassured me that he was confident this situation would be remedied before too long. Unlike a lot of men, Raymond looked forward to becoming a grandfather. He didn't see it as a sign of ageing but as a declaration of the continuation of his family.

Charles and Ve were of the same mind set and hoped their precious Anna would announce an engagement before too much longer or as they said to me in an aside, 'they were going to ask that boy what his intentions were.' They recognized the same wonderful qualities in Leo that I had. They also saw a young man that had been deprived of a loving family and they were eager to set that right.

I knew if Leo married their Anna he would become a true son to them and I could think of no one that deserved it more. While in the beginning I had looked on Leo as my son, I realized that our relationship would probably change when he married. Remembering Raymond's earlier cautions, I made up my mind not to be hurt when this happened because I'd always known you can't hold what doesn't want to be held. I had no doubt of his affection for me so saw no reason to strive to be first in his life. I knew how to love and at the same time let go and how important it was for future happiness and growth to a person. At long last he would finally have a place in his own family group when he married Anna and became Charles and Ve's son-in-law.

* * *

Next morning Raymond and I pulled onto the motorway just after breakfast. The weather report called for flurries later that evening but we planned to be home long before that. We stopped for a quick sandwich at noon and after a visit to the house and turning over the keys to the agent, were back on the road by one o'clock. An hour from home it began. The sky darkened and the temperature dropped drastically. The predicted rain descended as sleet and immediately froze upon contact with the tarmac. We and every other driver were travelling at sixty miles an hour on a sheet of ice. Everything happened so fast there was no time to adjust our speed. A kaleidoscope of shapes whirled before our eyes as car after car spun out of control. There was no avoiding the lorry careening directly towards us and upon impact we were propelled across the median straight into the path of oncoming traffic. All I can remember after that was the sound of sirens, flashing lights, and icy drops of snow dripping on my face; though I couldn't understand why it was red.

'Raymond,' I said, 'why is the snow red?'

'Don't worry about it Aggie it's going to be alright,' he answered. As his comforting voice reverberated in my ears I thought, Raymond's not worrying so why should I? Immediately the confusion of people and background noises began to fade as I ever so gently slipped into oblivion.

The next thing I was conscious of were faces hovering over me and blocking my view of Raymond. Damn I thought to myself, I wish they'd stop fussing and just let me sleep.

'Raymond, make them go away, please Raymond I'm so tired.'

'Aggie, Aggie, don't you damn well give up now you feisty woman.'

Why does Raymond sound annoyed with me I wondered?

'Raymond,' I called from what seemed a great distance, 'why are you angry with me?'

'I'm not angry but I want you to fight, just like you used to when we first met.'

I thought this a very strange request and answered, 'but why?'

'Never you mind why, just do it.'

'Is it what you really want Raymond?' I queried.

'Yes my dear Aggie, it's what I really want.'

I could hear somebody crying but when I tried to sit up to comfort them I realized I couldn't move. I think I remember saying, 'don't worry I'm going to help you, I just need a minute to get my breath.'

Sometime later I woke to find myself lying on a small moving bed, unable to sit up. When I asked for help a woman dressed in a white uniform leaned over me and told me I'd been in a motor accident and had a very narrow escape so I must try to lay still and not thrash about.

'Where's Raymond, where is my Raymond, is he alright?'

I was having difficulty focussing my eyes and when the woman in white didn't answer I thought she'd left the room. Thinking I'd look for Raymond myself I tried get off the bed, only to realize I was strapped down. Turning my head from side to side to see if there was anyone about to untie me I felt somebody give my arm a sharp pinch. Why did you do that, I wanted to ask? But even though I knew what I wanted to say I couldn't form the words and they were lost to me before I could rethink them. My last memory was confusion and frustration at not being able to move nor speak, then all at once it was over and I slipped peacefully into unconsciousness.

With the gradual return to awareness came the sense I was no longer alone, and as I opened and focussed my eyes, it was Raymond's face I saw looking down at me.

'Raymond, where have you been? They wouldn't tell me when I asked and then they made me sleep when I wanted to find you.'

'Aggie it's alright, everything is going to be alright.'

'Well I know that,' I answered a bit belligerently, 'you already said that when the rain was red.'

'My dear God I thank-you,' I heard him say, 'the feisty woman is back.'

It seemed Raymond's most serious injuries involved his neck and upper back. He was in a brace that restricted head movement and had been allowed to visit me only if he used a wheelchair. Naturally, we'd both received numerous minor injuries and massive bruising to just about every part of our bodies. My left leg was badly damaged and I was told later everyone thought I'd lose it. Thanks to the work of a brilliant bone surgeon and with lots of therapy I was told I'd walk again but would probably have to rely on the use of a stick. My personal care nurse told me when Raymond was informed he looked at the doctors and smiled saying, 'yes well, we'll just wait and see what she thinks about that.'

I had to remain in hospital after Raymond was discharged. Most of the time was spent in therapy, teaching me to strengthen different muscles till the damaged ones recovered from the trauma. A goodly amount of time was also spent on learning to do everyday tasks in a way that would prevent further stress, not only on my body but also on my mind. It seemed to me an undo amount of effort was spent on questions asking me how I felt about things. To my way of thinking this was nothing short of daft. How was one expected to feel about being involved in a car crash?

My main goal was to be well enough to return home to celebrate my very first Christmas with my new family. Everyone was wonderful about hospital visits and I never lacked for company but I just wanted to get back to a normal life. As much as I never felt neglected and was always kept abreast on all the family news, I was beginning to feel on the edge, just outside. I hadn't felt this way in a long time and knew if I could just be with Raymond the feelings would disappear. I begged, I pleaded and finally, in sheer frustration, I threatened to burn down the hospital if the doctor's didn't release me in time to spend the holidays at home.

Most times they looked at me in desperation because I wouldn't accept their advise on what they considered was in my best interest saying, 'My dear Ms Graymouse you must be patient.'

To which I'd respond, 'I'm not your dear Ms Graymouse and I'm telling you for the last bloody time before I do something you'll all live to regret, I want to go home now! Can't you understand that or are you too bloody thick?' Whereupon the inevitable end result of the argument culminated with me collapsing in tears, sorry I had given way and sorry I had lashed out at the very people responsible for saving my life. Nevertheless, while I was contrite I was not truly repentant.

December twenty second, my mother's birthday, I woke in a foul mood. It was apparent I hadn't swayed the medical staff to my way of thinking but I was still equally determined not to spend Christmas in hospital. Damnation, once again it's come to this I thought. I was going to have to take matters into my own hands and organize a plan of escape. As soon as breakfast was cleared away, beds remade and the ward given a tidy up, the patients set about falling into their day's routine. Careful not to draw undue attention to myself, I surreptitiously collected my few personal items and stashed them in the floppy cloth carrier bag Carley had brought filled with magazines and sweets. The sweets were long gone and now the magazines would become an effective camouflage for the oversize bag. Once in the waiting room I'd use the public telephone to call a taxi then casually continue my stroll down to the hospital entrance and wait for my ride. I secured my makeshift valise to my walking frame, collected the magazines and was about to begin my getaway when the therapist's aid arrived.

'You're going to go to therapy now instead of this afternoon Ms Graymouse.'

'And why is that?' I asked, attempting to conceal my irritation at being intercepted on the first stage of my journey.

'Sorry don't know. It's what Doctor told Matron so I'm here to take you down in the elevator.'

'I'm quite capable of using the elevator and getting myself to therapy,' I snapped at her.

'Don't know anything about that either Ms Graymouse, but when Matron gives an order I follow it and suggest you do the same.'

Damn, I knew who Matron was. She wasn't a large woman, a justifiable assumption if you regarded the way staff viewed her, to say nothing of their diligence in carrying out her orders. In fact she was quite the opposite, very petite, but tiny as she may have been in stature, she had a formidable bearing. Might even be a match for me I'd once thought, when I'd inadvertently overheard her give a royal dressing down to a nurse regarding the state of my bed covers.

Bloody cheek all this kowtowing but there seemed to be no point trying to reason with someone who insisted on following orders. It's so frustrating, all the while she's talking, and regardless of what I'm saying in reply, this minion continues to bundle me into the wheelchair preparing to follow her almighty Matron's orders. Some people are so damnably unreasonable I thought to myself, they'd try the patience of a saint and make a vicar swear.

There's nothing like a good physiotherapy workout to make you aware of your limitations and to-day my therapist seemed bound and determined to put me through my paces. Upon completion I wasn't so sure I had enough energy left to make it back to my room let alone make a furtive getaway. Maybe I'd have lunch and a short nap first. Actually come to think of it, that was a better time to avoid staff in the halls. The patients on my ward all tended to close their eyes for half an hour or so after lunch. Some of the nurses made use of this quiet time to visit the cafeteria for their meal while the remainder stayed at the nursing station taking an extra tea break. Perfect I decided, as my order obsessed warden got me tucked back into bed. All I had to do was rest a bit, recovering my strength as I waited for the approaching lunch trolleys, whose jangling clatter could even now be heard echoing down the halls.

I'd hardly finished lunch when Matron appeared on the ward. 'Ah Ms Graymouse,' she said, approaching my bed, 'I understand you are not happy with us.'

'Well,' I said somewhat taken aback by her unexpected presence and slightly confrontational manner, 'it's not that there is anything wrong with the hospital or anything like that it's just I've been here so long and I want to go home and be with my family at Christmas.'

'Hmm,' she mused, 'that doesn't seem an unreasonable request to me, why don't you phone someone to collect you and leave now?'

'Doctor hasn't signed me out,' I whined in a pathetic plea for her sympathy.

'Oh I see, and was that really going to prevent you from sneaking off when we weren't looking?'

It was another of the moments in my life when I couldn't think of a plausible reply so concentrating on keeping my jaw from gaping wide, while trying to feign ignorance of what possible reason there could be for such a question, I chose to say nothing. The ward was incredibly hushed and still, an aura of suspense hovered as we waited, but for what? Abruptly the silence was shattered as the twin doors were flung wide and Raymond entered pushing a wheel chair. All past attempts to keep my lower jaw fixed in place were defeated and it now dropped and hung slack, an open invitation to any passing fly to wander in.

The entire ward broke into gales of laughter, the younger nurses even clapping their hands in their excitement. 'We knew, we knew,' they chanted, 'even Matron knew what you had planned.'

Matron looked at me as I imagine she would have observed an errant child and said, 'I told Doctor I thought the time at home would be more beneficial than staying in hospital over the holidays when therapy would be cut to a minimum anyway. He agreed and signed you out so you're free to go on the understanding you're faithful to your exercises and particularly that you don't get overtired.'

I grasped her tiny hand in mine and said with sincere and heartfelt joy, 'Merry Christmas Matron and the Happiest New Year ever.'

Looking somewhat pleased but unaccustomed at this show of affection, she quickly retrieved her hand as the patients joined with the nurses and began to clap again saying 'well done Matron, well done.' Her pleasure at being thanked in such an open manner was obvious but temporarily caused her to lose her composure. In an attempt to restore decorum in spite of flushed cheeks, she mumbled something about it being time to get on with more pressing duties. Nobody was deceived by this and she knew it so in a last attempt to recover her usual demeanour, she bid me a very formal good-bye and departed, leaving me to the ministrations of her staff. Immediately they gathered about, dressing me, asking me if there was anything else I needed, and questioning did I have everything. Finally bundled up as neatly as a pig in a blanket and safely secured in the wheel chair, my young nurse pushed me from bed to bed giving me time to say good-bye to all the patients of whom I'd grown so fond of.

Seat belt on and muffled in car robes we made our way home. I was already beginning to feel the effects of my busy morning. By the time we reached the hotel I realized how totally draining the move and trip had been. I was genuinely exhausted and, not for the last time would be aware of how much I had come to rely upon the daily, orderly routine of the hospital. Without my knowing, it was the reason I thought I could handle everything as I had before the accident. How wrong I was. Though grateful to be released in time for Christmas, there would be times I would long for the protection of hospital procedures. The expectations of nursing staff that I would allow their ministrations had relieved me of all decision making. I had doctors and specialists to thank for my life, but I knew I had the nursing sisters and physiotherapists to thank for my recovery.

As soon as we reached the hotel, I asked to go to my room telling everyone I would keep my word to Matron and have a short rest. If I'm honest I must admit it had nothing to do with earlier promises to Matron, it was a necessity. Fully clothed I lay on the bed and was nearly asleep when I felt a warm cosy quilt being tucked under my chin. Hours later I woke to hear carols being softly played in the background and lifting my head from the pillow, saw Raymond sitting in his favourite chair. Everything seemed to be as it should and I flitted in and out of a hazy sleep. Time did not seem to be of any consequence, it just was.

The next thing I knew was being gently woken by Carley and asked if I was ready for something to eat. I soon discovered I was not only ravenous but re-energized. Feeling well rested I thoroughly enjoyed the quiet meal and conversation with Raymond before the rest of the family joined us for coffee and Christmas cake. Anna conveyed her best wishes on my homecoming but said her parents would wait till I'd had time to adjust to the move before they visited. There were cards to open from tradespeople, neighbours and so many others wishing me well and it all contributed to feeling cherished, safe, and home at last in every way.

Bed time finally arrived and as much as I was longing to fall asleep in Raymond's arms it wasn't to be, not yet anyway. Anna and Carley helped me into my night gown made sure I took my pain medication and lovingly tucked me into bed. My earlier energy level had suddenly plummeted again and though longing for sleep, I couldn't get comfortable and twisted and turned, searching for the right spot. Raymond entered the room and as he approached the bed saw my discomfort.

'Aggie I'm going to lie down on the sofa. I'll be close if you need anything in the night so remember you won't be alone. You've had a long day and it's no wonder you're restless and experiencing a little difficulty. Try to relax till your pain medication takes effect, it won't be long and believe me, a good night's rest will make all the difference.'

I didn't argue because by this time after what was to me a marathon day, all I wanted to do was close my eyes. Once again I remembered how the enforced hospital routine had contributed greatly to my feelings of well-being. How could I show my appreciation and thank them all I wondered, but my weary mind rebelled at yet another request to concentrate. Mercifully it shut down in the brief pause between breaths and I was free again, sleeping undisturbed throughout the night.

Chapter Seventeen

The twenty-third of December brought a heavy snowfall to all of North Yorkshire. The roads became impassable as the temperature dropped drastically and wet snow froze where it fell. Very much like the day of our accident. It stirred memories, but not the usual kind. I seemed to be recalling things that until then I'd either forgotten or had never been aware of happening at all.

'Raymond,' I said, as we sat finishing a last cup of coffee at breakfast, 'I think I'm remembering things now that I didn't know happened, and it frightens me.'

'Aggie you got a good shaking up when that lorry collided so I don't think it's unreasonable to expect some disjointed memories.'

'Do you have them too?' I asked.

'Strange thoughts yes, but I don't let them worry me and I think you should try to do the same. Just attribute it to the trauma you experienced and try not to dwell on it. The less importance you attach to them the sooner they'll fade.'

I didn't question him further but was not completely satisfied with his answer. Something else happened, I don't know how I knew but I just knew.

The next day I had time to really take in my surroundings. The hotel looked so festive. Richard and Carley had done a fantastic job with decorating and with almost a full house, everyone joined in the spirit of the season. Some of the guests had expected to be home for Christmas day but now wouldn't risk driving because of weather conditions. Nevertheless they accepted what couldn't be changed and embraced the opportunity for a new experience. Rushing to the little village shop to buy whatever was for sale, so as not to deny their partner a gift, they purchased packets of biscuits, chocolates, and even one conscientious wife bought her husband a package of Brillo pads because he'd promised to help with the washing up this year. For the first time in a long while I was eagerly anticipating the festivities.

It was Christmas Eve, always my favourite time of the holiday season. When my children were young all the special baking was put out, other treats, bought only for the holiday were in abundance, and the theme was certainly one of excess without any of the usual accompanying guilt. It was also the last chance to slip secret presents under the tree before morning. Sometime later when all were asleep Father Christmas would arrive and the myth would be complete. It was Christmas, the ultimate time of sharing, the way it was meant to be and it was wonderful. Sadly for me when my sons married they ignored our family traditions and cheerfully allowed themselves to be absorbed into the customs of their in-laws and what had once been the most wonderful night of the year for me, became a night of loneliness. To salve their conscience they made appearances to varying degrees but I was never included as a part of their Christmas in the true sense of the word. The attempts to pacify me with whatever times remained after arranging their real Christmas around their wives families were obvious, and I was always aware of the feeble rehearsed dialogue intended to manipulate me into thinking I had a say in when they'd visit. I could have borne the shame and pain better had they not insulted my intelligence. It would have been kinder had they just totally ignored me instead. Definitely not the end of the world but when the grandchildren arrived, well then it became unforgivable.

But this night before Christmas would be different. I would be with people young and old who loved me and wanted me in their lives, to share their lives, not just to-night but always. I would be with my Raymond who cherished me, warts and all. I couldn't help but think I must have done something right over the years to now have this wonderful man in my life.

I went to my room around three o'clock and lay down for a nap. As much as I wanted to be in the midst of the excitement every moment of the day I knew I still tired easily, and after all had been done to make this Christmas the best ever, I did not want to be the one to put a damper on the festivities because I had not made an effort to at least be well rested. Even Charles and Ve had gone to considerable trouble and expense arranging for extra help to manage the pub so they could join us to celebrate our first Christmas Eve together as a family. By eight o'clock we were all gathered in the main dining room and mixing with the hotel guests.

Richard and Leo had organized and paid for a Christmas Eve happy hour consisting of a table overloaded with every imaginable nibble and a free glass of champagne for all. When it came time for a toast the two boys along with Carley and Anna put their arms over each other's shoulders and with me in the centre, we raised our glasses toasting present company, absent friends and loved ones. A most beautiful honour to all I thought and lifting my glass I felt Raymond draw me closer, then pressing his lips to my ear he ever so softly whispered, 'absent friends and loved ones.'

Later we invited Charles and Ve to join us, leaving the younger ones to cater to the guests, most of which chose to remain in the public area rather than return to their rooms. Opening the door to our lounge we were greeted by the little artificial tree I'd dressed in sparkling miniature lights and which now created spiralling halos in the frost covered windows, reflecting back our own private Aura Borealis. The room was cast in a warm, welcoming glow in contrast to the outdoors. The bitter, blasting wind from the north had at last subsided and now only light snow fell lazily, muffling all sound as it caressed and smoothed out the ragged windblown drifts. Outdoor lights lit up dark corners of the garden and as the feathery white flakes rested on evergreen boughs, all was transformed to become a living Christmas card scene of beauty. The worst of the weather seemed to be over.

At eleven o'clock Charles and Ve called for their previously booked cab. There were hugs all around accompanied by boisterous wine induced shouts, reminding all that we'd meet again to-morrow at dinner. Closing the door I realized I was once again drained. I'd felt Raymond's eyes on me more than once during the evening but when I questioned him he just said he liked looking at me and what was wrong with that? It made me laugh and I couldn't tell him I didn't want him to look at me so I forgot about it till now. I wondered if he was worried about me, and if he was, why?

At last the evening had drawn to a close and I was only too glad to go to my bedroom. As soon as I entered the room Raymond excused himself saying I should get into bed and he'd be back in a few minutes. I didn't need any persuading as the thought of lying down was more than a little appealing. I may have dozed off for a moment or maybe I dreamed it because suddenly Raymond was in the room, pushing a cloth covered bulky object before him.

'What is that, why are you bringing it in here,' I said?

'You'll see in a minute, don't be so impatient to know everything. Some people like to have secrets you know.'

'Oh yes, well just tell me so I can go to sleep.'

'How shocking to hear those words coming from your lips. I tell you, it's a sad state of affairs when a man wants to lie next to the woman he loves and all she can think about is sleep! You're a hard woman Ms Graymouse'

And then as he removed the cover I realized what he'd wheeled into the room. It was a folding cot, the kind used for an extra guest in a family room. Lining it up alongside my bed he proceeded to make it up with sheets and pillows.

'It's Christmas Eve my Nessie and I want to sleep with you.' It brought back the memory of the first time he'd said that to me but this time I moved from the middle of my bed closer to the edge. I said nothing, just like the other time, but pulled the duvet across to cover his bed then folded it back and waited for him.

Rays of what I can only describe as celestial light streamed through the window, proclaiming to our small world in North Yorkshire it was Christmas morning. Carefully getting out of bed I wrapped my dressing gown around me and slowly made my way to the window without using my walking frame. The snow in the garden, once a soft blanket, was now crisp from the overnight frost. Shards of bright sunshine filtered through the shrubbery and as it highlighted the stark, frozen surface, it became almost painfully bright to look upon. It was a Christmas morning to rival a dream.

'Merry Christmas my Nessie,' I turned to see Raymond now awake and watching me. 'Come back to bed woman.'

Slowly making my way back to bed to lay by his side I said, 'Merry Christmas my Raymond, I love you.'

'Hmm, I guess if I'd ever needed any convincing I wouldn't after last night would I?' he said.

'Oh are you sure,' I teased, 'maybe I could have done better.'

'Well now, that certainly sounds like an invitation.'

This was not going as I hoped so I said, 'Raymond I think I hear somebody at the door.' As he looked towards the door I got out of bed as quickly as I could and said, 'control yourself man, you're turning into a wild beast.'

Raymond still had to move gingerly and he knew that once I was out of bed he couldn't get me back in.

'Alright,' he conceded, 'I'll let you off this time but only this once.'

I made coffee and took a cup to Raymond before I went to shower. Drying off I could hear him get out of bed so dressed at once before he got any more wild ideas. Fully clothed I went into the kitchen and started breakfast while Raymond showered. Later, sitting by the window watching robins and various other small birds at the bird station Raymond said, 'shall we exchange our gifts now before the day gets too hectic?

'Yes lets,' I answered, 'especially since it's not exactly a surprise as we've worn them since November.'

Earlier we had decided to buy each other identical gold chains and St. Christopher medals for Christmas. St Christopher being the patron saint of travellers, we thought it appropriate to exchange them the day we left my little house for the last time; a symbol of the beginning of our own special journey together. Last night we had taken them off and wrapped each separately in tissue to wait an official exchange on Christmas morning. Now Raymond went to the dresser to retrieve them. Removing the tissue paper from my gift he kissed the medal and fastened the chain about my neck saying, 'wear this forever my Nessie.'

I gazed at the disc as it lay glowing on my skin between my breasts and answered, 'I will my love.'

Then I put Raymond's chain around his neck and secured the clasp. With the golden disc lying nestled in his greying chest hair I said, 'wear this forever my Raymond,' and bending forward kissed both his chest and the medal. True to his lecherous mind set this morning, he immediately responded with, 'hey I didn't get to do that, now it's my turn.'

Laughing at his empty promises to behave if I'd just let him get close enough to kiss me, I knew better, so kept well out of his reach.

After we tidied the kitchen and made the beds I waited in our suite as Raymond went in search of the boys. True to their duties, Richard was at reception and Leo was in the kitchen. Anna had donned a hotel apron and was assisting Carley with serving and taking breakfast orders. Raymond let the staff know he was on call for anything that might require his assistance and returned to escort me from our suite.

With my arm linked through Raymond's and his hand enclosing mine, we made our way through the foyer and into the public lounge where we were greeted with exuberant wishes for a Merry Christmas, accompanied by hugs and kisses from employees and guests alike. I felt Raymond tense then give my hand a short, sharp squeeze and I knew he was as overcome with emotion as I. For a brief moment out of time, our gaze locked, reflecting tear filled eyes on the brink of overflowing. Then as suddenly as it had arrived, the interlude passed and we returned to the present and began offering our greetings with enthusiasm and sincerity.

I've always thought the feelings of love and good will expressed during the Christmas season, more than any other time, have throughout the ages been a catalyst for change and a time to heal past wounds. Those of a more cynical nature and mind set could perceive it as hypocritical, but for many of us it holds the hope that not only is it the true meaning of the season, but holds the underlying, unspoken promise that one day it will become what it was created for, not just for our Christmas time but for our lifetime.

Raymond and I had decided we would not buy the boys personal gifts. What they most needed and wanted was money for their business venture. They had opened a joint bank account and had a contract drawn up by a specialist in business law after Raymond and I discussed their proposal of a partnership and given them our blessing. We decided ten thousand pounds between them was a reasonable amount. Raymond had suggested twenty till I reminded him that maybe weddings weren't too far in the future. For Carley and Anna we chose a voucher to a London hotel offering the girls a weekend of festivities and pampering in their famous spa. Our employees were given cash bonuses, the amount dependent on their length of service. Raymond was a demanding but generous employer so most of the staff had been with him a long time. Bottles of wine and vouchers to be used at the Chapel and Chimes were for Charles and Ve. As publicans they both enjoyed being served well prepared food. Leo would introduce them to Chef Aidan thus assuring them an extra treat. Chef had a particular way of treating Raymond's guests as though they were royalty and his special treatment would not go appreciated by Charles and Ve.

As per the usual Christmas day schedule, hotel guests would be served at dinner at three o'clock. Once coffee and desert had been consumed, each guest would receive a secret Santa bag containing a small bottle of wine, crisps, biscuits, cheese, selection of nuts and dried fruit, all intended to carry them over till breakfast when normal service would resume. Barring emergencies, Raymond insisted his staff not be disturbed as they enjoy their own dinner, whether they chose to have it at the hotel or elsewhere. We would be dining around six or as close to that time as Richard and Leo could manage so Charles and Ve would arrive any time after five. Raymond and I both decided to take a rest between two and four as it would probably be another late evening. I fell into a deep sleep and had to be woken by Carley telling me it was time to get up and dress for dinner. Again I must have been more tired than I thought. Raymond had been up for some time and was bustling about the suite, making sure all was ready for our guests.

'Raymond why didn't you wake me so I could help you?' I asked.

'Wasn't much to do Aggie. Besides an ancient, old, crone of a woman like you needed her sleep, that's why.'

He deftly sidestepped as I threw the cushion, then to add further insult to injury, he had the temerity to laugh as it careened into the table lamp, nearly toppling it. Utter waste of time and energy, it only caused the daft bugger to laugh even more.

Dinner and the evening itself was a truly unforgettable experience. Leo did the cooking and presented the food family style so we could serve ourselves allowing everyone to enjoy the food together. Used dishes were placed in a plastic container and put out of sight till to-morrow; when they would be washed in the hotel dishwasher. The remainder of the evening was spent in our lounge. Gifts given and received, wine drunk, toasts proposed, hugs and laughter, a few tears of happiness and an abundance of gratitude, in thanksgiving for the true gift of the day.

* * *

The next few days passed routinely and uneventfully. As the roads cleared hotel guests checked out, taking the opportunity to visit friends on their way home. It had become a tradition a few years back, when Raymond's wife was still with him and Richard had become old enough to want to celebrate, for Raymond to close down the hotel for New Year's Eve and New Year's Day, a very generous concession to his staff. Most had worked extra hours and given their all over the Christmas season so this was a bonus for a job well done. This worked equally well for Raymond and me also. Neither of us cared much about the last day of the year in terms of a party so were happy to stay put. This left the younger set to their own devices of searching out favourite venues to see out the old and bring in the new, while leaving us in peace and quiet.

Chapter Eighteen

It had been a wonderful Christmas but as usual at this time of year, time moved forward in a state of anti-climax holiday leftovers. As each day followed the last I knew that while I was gaining bodily strength I could not dismiss the disturbing feeling that something was still not right. A cloud was hanging over me and I could no longer ignore it. A feeling that around the time of the accident, something else had happened which I couldn't remember. So I braced myself to ask the question I knew must be asked. With hope of being able to accept the answer, I lay my book aside and said 'Raymond I have to ask you something and can't put it off any longer. After the accident I think something happened to me but now I can't remember what it was. I think you know and I want you to tell me about it.'

Taking my hand in his he proceeded to tell me in a calm and straightforward way that my heart had kicked up a bit of a fuss when I was having my leg operated on. The doctor's felt it needed a bit of tending to and that I would certainly benefit from a procedure that was now becoming everyday surgery. Well damn, and another damn. That sneaky old atrial fibrillation fluttering that I'd had for who knows how long, had reared its ugly head again. Raymond said the tension in the operating theatre had been so high at one point that no one could decide if my heart was going to return to a steady beat, or maybe stop for a permanent rest. Of course in the end it resumed a more or less steady rhythm which why I'm here to-day just as big as life. In one way it was a relief to have my feelings validated but it also stirred up memories of another time, reminding me of other days when I had been exploited and made a fool of.

'So Raymond is everyone waiting for me to die?' I asked.

'Aggie you're not going to die any sooner or later than anyone else.'

'What the hell does that mean?' I shot back.

'Simply this, now that you're aware of the situation and physically stronger, you're going to return to the hospital and have a pacemaker inserted to regulate your heartbeat and do away with those irksome flutters you experience.'

I could feel my anger rising, had I being deceived, made to look the fool again? 'And why wasn't I told before?' I demanded.

'The specialist said you had already suffered enough mental and physical trauma due to the accident and it would be best for you if we waited till you were stronger before telling you and causing you further stress.'

I knew this was the truth but at the back of my mind lurked a fear, or maybe it was more than a fear, was it a premonition? Was I meant to die on the operating table after all? After much soul searching I reached the decision this was one of those life happenings that already was. I had no control over the event nor the outcome and just this once it would be best for all if I gracefully accepted the inevitable and got on with it without the usual battles.

Two weeks later on the last day of January, I was due for a check-up at the hospital. The orthopaedic surgeon said my leg had healed as well as any forty year old to which I relied, 'and why should it not, when that's just my age?' He left laughing and shaking his head saying he wished all his patients were just like me.

In my heart of hearts I had every reason to doubt that. I distinctly remember one morning when the pain was especially bad. My medication wasn't due for another thirty minutes at the time he arrived for rounds. After a moments chat with me I received my injection; possibly his watch was set a little ahead of the nurse's time piece or possibly he thought I was quite capable of carrying out whatever I was threatening him with at that particular moment.

Then it was on to the heart man for a serious consultation. I swear my behaviour was more than reasonable until he made reference to, 'someone of your advanced years.'

Raymond of course had accompanied me and it was then I heard him inhale sharply and mutter two words, 'oh no.'

Eventually Raymond managed to calm me down and I saw the heart surgeon look at him in what I can only describe as sympathy as he offered his apologies, adding he didn't realize I was so sensitive, which of course set me off on another tangent. Finally I conceded to listen and he went on to describe the procedure and the prognosis.

'Hmm,' I said, looking him straight in the eye when he had finished speaking, 'that's providing that at my advanced years I bloody well survive.'

With relief on his face at escaping without hospital security being called, Raymond got me into the car. Before he switched on the ignition he looked directly at me and said, 'did you have to be so bloody minded?'

'No I did not,' I answered, 'but it sure felt good.'

Surgery was scheduled for February thirteenth, my youngest son's birthday, and I was checked in on the twelfth for pre surgery tests and monitoring. Certainly I was apprehensive but not wringing my hands in despair. I'd made life much easier for myself since I'd accepted that because some things already were, it didn't make much sense to fret over them. Simple for some maybe, but it had taken me a lifetime to learn. I could have saved myself a lot of distress if I'd grasped the fact sooner but in this case it was surely better late than never.

It was early morning and while staff were making final preparations I was waiting for the boys to arrive. They had promised to stop in for a quick good-bye and it was just minutes before they were due when a nurse noticed the gold chain and medal still about my neck.

'Oh Ms Graymouse, you'll have to remove your jewellery before you go into theatre.'

'I'm not taking this off,' I informed them, as I grasped the gold disc in my fist.

'But Ms...'

'Understand this here and now, I'm not going to theatre or anywhere else if I have to take this off so if that's the case you can get my clothes and I won't keep you any longer,' and once said I made to get out of bed.

'Ms Graymouse please, you mustn't upset yourself, Doctor is on his way.'

'Then I suggest you bloody well tell Doctor that I'm on my way too,' I replied, swinging my legs over the edge of the bed.

Just then the boys arrived. Looking to them for support the nurse asked, 'Oh will you please make Ms Graymouse understand she can't wear jewellery into theatre. She says she's leaving if she has to remove it and her blood pressure is rising dangerously.'

At this moment the surgeon also saw fit to put in an appearance and wanted to know what all the commotion was about. Richard approached me saying, 'Aggie, what is it you want to keep with you?' I opened my fist and Richard gazed down at the golden disc in the palm of my hand. He looked long and hard into my eyes, then touching my shoulder in comfort said, 'don't worry Aggie, I'll have a word.'

Gesturing to the surgeon he indicated he wanted a private moment and they walked to the far side of the room. They spoke for a minute or two and returning to my bedside the surgeon looked at the nurse, 'Sister, leave the chain and medal on Ms Graymouse but wrap them in sterile gauze and let's not upset our patient any further.'

The now thoroughly confused nurse proceeded to do as asked while the Doctor turned his attention on me. 'Ms Graymouse, I'm flaunting hospital policy for you and I expect something in return.'

'What would that be?' I asked, a mite suspiciously.

'I want you to swear that from this moment forward you will concede to every request the staff make of you and personally promise me, on your honour, that you'll make a quick recovery and stay so healthy that I may never have to treat you again.'

The last he tempered with a smile and I answered, 'yes sir, Mr Fairley, I certainly will be a model patient if I can, I promise you.'

'Well that's good enough for me, let's get to theatre.' Looking about and addressing everyone in the room he said, 'say your good-byes people'

Giving my shoulder a gentle squeeze he said, 'I'll be with you shortly Ms Graymouse,' then promptly left the room.

After the boys had left I was given a preoperative sedative and soon was being wheeled down a long, dim corridor. My mind wandered back and forth flitting from daydreams to a very hazy reality. Raymond's face was always before me but gradually it began to fade from my sight. 'Raymond,' I called out, 'where are you going?'

'I'm right here Nessie right beside you as always, you know that don't you?'

'Yes Raymond, I know that,' I answered.

I came through surgery with flying colours and in high spirits. I felt sure my good feelings could be attributed to being able to breathe without those rapid fluttering heartbeats followed by gasps of breathlessness. Richard and Leo came to visit me but when I asked where Raymond was there was a moment of uncomfortable silence, as though I was expecting a bit too much to have them all there at the same time.

'Oh of course,' I said, somewhat embarrassed at my selfishness, 'someone has to keep the business running, forgive me, how could I have forgotten.'

'Nessa…,' Leo began.

But he was interrupted in mid sentence by Richard saying, 'you'll be coming home in a day or so, is there anything you want till then?'

'No nothing at all but I am drowsy, guess it's due to the anaesthetic.' The boys nodded their heads in agreement but said no more, just kissed me good-bye and left.

Chapter Nineteen

I had a dream that night, although while it was happening I didn't know it was a dream, it was reality and the time was now. It was about Raymond and he came to me. I still remember feeling an unworldly sense of time out of time that I could actually see him but, I immediately dismissed it because of the joy I felt. My elation was short lived, quickly replaced by a sense that at last I would know the truth, the real truth that until now had been hidden from me, a truth, my truth. A validation that my truth was real and what I had been deceived into believing was a horrible nightmare. Immediately it began playing out like a film on fast forward, each scene flicked by scarcely allowing time to make sense of it before another flashed before my eyes. Or maybe it was before it became imprinted on my mind, because vision and thought seemed to be one and occur simultaneously. Suddenly his face was before me, enveloping my entire vision. I felt my body, heart and soul struggle to focus on the significance of what was happening and even more importantly, on what was about to happen. I couldn't take my eyes from his face, feeling a great need to engrave his image in my memory forever. Frozen in this single-minded state of desperation I continued to search for meaning, perhaps hidden within his features. Unwilling or unable, he said nothing until at last no longer capable of bearing the strain I heard myself say, 'Raymond they said you were dead.'

As I spoke the words the significance of their meaning created such a sense of exhilaration in me. By voicing my thoughts aloud it refuted what I was supposed to believe. They had been wrong and I had been right all along. He was alive and well and at that moment I felt a great sense of rebirth, everything would be as it was. Before, had been only a dreadful mistake and this was the proof. His eyes now bore into mine, as if he too needed to absorb me entirely in his gaze. Yet he still hesitated to speak, as he sometimes did when he needed my reassurance I wanted to hear the truth, no matter the consequences. Finally in what seemed an eternity, in a calm and matter of fact way he spoke, 'I am,' he said.

His words stunned me and I couldn't believe what I'd heard. Why would he say such a thing? I could only remain chained and shackled in the nightmarish state of being unable to move or flee and I was forced to witness what happened next. Feelings of overwhelming disappointment and distress flowed through my mind, culminating with the certainty of a far greater agony, yet to be endured. Then ever so slowly as if to reinforce these feelings, Raymond's face began to alter till it manifested as a waxen image. It became elongated, his features twisted and distorted as they began to drip, melding, and molding, till at last his face was totally beyond recognition. Then I was to experience the final horror, he disappeared before my eyes.

Even to this day if I dwell on that period, without my volition I begin to relive those feelings of terror as I woke from the nightmare, still screaming at the truth as it penetrated my conscious mind, 'he's dead, he's dead, he's been dead all along,' Then to complete the circle I screamed into the mind of God to tell him I finally understood.

After, I really have no idea how long after, I was aware I was no longer in the hospital but back in our suite at the hotel. No, there was no happy, homecoming welcome because Raymond was not there to enfold me in his arms. My Raymond had been killed outright in the crash, his neck had been broken and he died instantly.

With the help of Doctor's and particularly my loved ones I was made to understand that I hadn't been able to face losing him and had withdrawn into my own world where he and I were still together. Since the accident I had experienced many flashbacks that eventually helped me to gather and process information till finally I was able to accept the reality. They say conversations I thought I had with Raymond are mixed with conversations with Doctor's, advising not to force memories and that I would remember when I was physically and mentally ready to handle it. They told me many times I attributed Richard's suggestions as Raymond's wishes; especially regarding the Christmas holiday. Richard was my life support in every way and truly his Father's son. Finally, when he deemed me ready, he showed me a report he'd received from the surgeon that had allowed me to keep my chain and medal during the heart surgery. It said, 'considering her age and the extent of the physical injuries incurred, healing has been remarkable. Granted she has not yet come to terms regarding the loss of your father but fortunately, in her favour is a tenacious will to overcome adversity. I believe this is what, given time, will allow her spirit to heal also. My own recommendation is that you allow her to determine when she is capable of accepting the loss.'

Gradually with continued love and support I've healed both physically and mentally and entered into a new stage of life. A stage of life as far as others are concerned, is without Raymond. There is absolutely no point in attempting to explain to Richard and the others I know my Raymond has not left me. I'm sure they'd all be of the same opinion that I was slipping back into that fantasy world where I existed after the accident. For instance, just this Christmas morning past, as I sat with my coffee and watched the birds around the bird station, I knew Raymond was watching with me. No, of course I didn't see him with my eyes but he was there all the same. And no, I was not just recalling something we had once shared. I tell you, he was there. I can't explain it to my own self so wouldn't expect Richard or anyone else to understand it either. In time I've learned not to fret nor question such things, it simply no longer matters. This is another one of those issues that 'just are.' Thinking realistically most of us can't say we know how radio, computer and many other things work but we know they do and they make our lives richer whether we understand the technology or not. From my point of view I've come to the conclusion, you don't have to know how or why, you just accept, appreciate, and serenity is restored.

Two years have passed since the accident and it has been a happy and hectic time. Richard and Leo married their girls and both young women are now expecting babies. Anna is having twins so I suspect Ve and myself will be much in demand for babysitting duties. Carley's baby is due a month earlier and they're hoping for a boy. What joy this will give Raymond. How we looked forward to the day when he'd hold his grandchild; but for now he'll have to be content that it will be me holding his precious babe.

I've had no further heart problems and the Doctor's swear I'll outlive them all to which I reply, 'ah yes, they say only the good die young and I hold you personally responsible to see it stays that way.'

I've developed a bit of arthritis in my damaged leg but consider myself lucky to be able to walk with only a slight limp and without the use of a stick. I make myself useful around the hotel and as Richard tells it, I entertain the guests in exchange for a leaky roof over my head and a daily morsel of stale bread.

My Leo is now a fully qualified head chef and equal business partner with Richard, who has also excelled, acquiring his managerial diploma with top marks. Living their dream they are content and happy working together with their families as entwined as the family business. The partnership agreement that Raymond had drawn up when they first stated their intent still serves them well.

Charles and Ve are getting weary of the pub business and have decided to sell after giving Leo first offer. They always knew cooking was his great love but because he is their much treasured son-in-law, wanted to give him first refusal. Anna was more than happy at his decision to remain a chef as she did not want to be directly involved in his day to day work. She looked forward to the time she'd be a stay at home Mum with her children and husband a priority. Something she'd not always felt because of the necessity of her parent's commitment to the long hours and hard work necessary to running a profitable pub. For Anna the welfare of her husband and children would always come first and for someone from Leo's background and childhood history, she represented an angel in disguise. From Leo's point of view, no matter the demands of being head chef, his wife and children would never experience the disinterest or lack of attention and affection that had coloured his life. His children would be encouraged to become all they could be and would never feel they were on the outside looking in.

Last but not Final Chapter

To-day when I woke my first thought was how interesting life really is and how true it is that, 'what goes around comes around.' I guess these thoughts have been brought to mind again since I've come to realize how very much Richard is his father's son.

At Raymond's funeral service, of which I have no memory at all, Richard's Mother attended by herself. The man she'd given up her marriage and son for had walked out long ago and according to Richard, she'd had numerous liaisons since. She told her son she regretted her actions and hoped that one day he might forgive her. With no malice in his heart at all Richard replied he would let her know when that day arrived but until then sincerely wished her well. Richard also showed me a letter of condolence my sons had sent after Raymond's death was published in the papers. The gist of it was; they apologized but unfortunately couldn't attend the service and hoped I'd understand. I told Richard to dispose of the letter as it had no meaning or sentiment for me and would not be placed in the book of condolences. I can no longer be hurt by them so they have no hold over me. In regard to their offspring, my grandchildren, I've even come to terms with that situation. The realization that had my life not been the way it was, I would never have made the decisions I did so would not be where I am to-day. That knowledge alone has offered a freedom from the past and all the accompanying pain. To-day it is unthinkable that I should never have met Raymond. Becoming part of his life and those who love me for myself, has given true meaning to my life, it fulfilled my destiny.

It was the last day of September when Raymond's grandson entered our world. He was in my arms and I was telling him he was the most beautiful and most wanted baby ever, when it happened. I felt Raymond's presence so strongly that I immediately looked to Richard and Carley, wondering why they didn't say something.

They were smiling contentedly while I held their precious son. Seemingly oblivious to the fact that Raymond stood by my side, one hand resting on my shoulder while his grandson clasped a finger of his other hand in a cherub fist. Knowing it would serve no useful purpose to say Raymond was with us again, I said nothing. Instead I surrendered to and embraced the feeling of our love and togetherness again.

To celebrate and honour, rather than mourn his father's life, Richard and Carley chose the third anniversary of the accident for their son's christening. Royston Leonard Gordon was duly accepted into the church amid gurgles of happiness as the holy water dripped from his head onto his cheeks. Royston was both Raymond and Richard's second name so it seemed appropriate this child should carry it also. Much to our combined joy Leo and I were chosen to be godparents. It was during my recovery days that Leo and I became more open about our feelings, not only in regards to each other but also about the impact Raymond had on our lives. We would be forever joined in our love for him so becoming godparents to his grandson was just another cementing and comformation of that relationship.

A christening tea was held at the hotel later that afternoon and the newest member to the Gordon clan was handed about and admired by all; as was Leo and Anna's twin girls, now six week old. Charles and Ve couldn't seem to get enough of their granddaughters and paraded them about as if they themselves had been the producers of the darling twosome.

Royston received some lovely christening gifts that were opened during the tea in order to thank each giver personally. However I chose to present the gift from his grandfather and me when it was quieter, when there were just Richard, Carley and myself present.

By five o'clock all the guests had left for home and we three with Royston returned to my suite. I made coffee and opened a bottle of champagne to toast the little man of the hour and his parents. This was something Raymond would have done and the sense of his presence was so intense to-day I didn't have to think about what to do, I just did what I knew to be right. After I proposed the toast to Royston and his parents, Richard returned a toast that brought tears to my eyes, 'present company, absent friends and loved ones.' Repeating the words and raising our glasses to drink, was when I saw him. Raymond standing over the small cot I kept for Royston, glass held high looking down lovingly at his grandson before looking to me and repeating the words, 'absent friends and loved ones.'

'What is it Aggie?' Richard asked, as I quickly sat down.

'Are you alright?' said Carley, coming to sit next to me.

'Yes, yes of course I am, just a bit of an emotional day for an old crock like me. Look at that son of yours you'd swear he's staring at someone wouldn't you? He's entranced.'

I got up and walked over to the dresser and removed a packet wrapped in tissue paper. 'Richard and Carley, this is a gift to Royston, it's from his grandfather and me. We exchanged Christmas gifts early that year but didn't tell anyone. On Christmas Eve we took these off and officially exchanged them again Christmas morning.'

Richard's face was transformed into a mask. Concern and worry were stamped on his features, his brow furrowed with the fear of unknown questions yet to be asked and answered.

'Aggie, do you want to have a rest?'

'No dear, why should I? You mustn't fuss over me, I told you it was just an emotional moment but I'm fine, anyway, this is our gift.' I undid the tissue wrapped packet and lay the gold chain and St. Christopher medal on Royston's small chest.

'Where did you get that Aggie?' said Richard softly as he came toward me.

'Why I just told you dear, this is the matching medal and chain that your father and I exchanged that Christmas morning.'

'Aggie, you know Dad was not alive then.'

'Hmm, well yes I do Richard but it's not mine, here's mine,' and I brought it forth from round my neck for their inspection.

Richard looked to Carley and said, 'you saw it Carley, you saw it in the safe this morning when I removed Dad's signet ring to wear at the christening.'

'I did Richard but what's to account for the fact that it is now lying on our son's chest?'

'Aggie, do you know the combination to my safe?'

'Of course not Richard, I never even knew the combination when it was your Dad's safe, it wasn't necessary.'

'My dearest Aggie, I don't want to upset you but you need to know I removed this from Dad's neck when I had to identify him at the morgue. Since then it has been locked in my safe. I was waiting for the day you'd ask about it and then return it to you; how did you come by it?'

'Richard I have no idea, it was in the drawer wrapped in tissue, I don't know how long it's been there I just know I was to give it to Royston.'

'There must be some explanation,' said Richard.

Carley picked up her son and looking towards her husband said, 'does it really matter? His grandfather wanted him to have it and his godmother has seen those wishes carried out.'

Richard walked towards his wife and son and wrapping an arm about my waist drew me close within their circle. 'No it doesn't matter, the only thing that matters is we are all here now, together again.'

It was then I knew I was being offered another adventure, this time with my loving family's support and I couldn't see how I could possibly refuse the invitation.

Epilogue

Is it feasible to entertain the thought that all children come into the world with a belief in an afterlife? Could it be, during their formative years, the outer world invades their inner sanctum causing them to suffer a temporary amnesia of what they once knew? And finally coming full circle, whether through ageing or life events, those seemingly forgotten beliefs are then re-experienced as flashbacks or intuition? Parallel universes, beings of energy, heaven, reincarnation, fate, destiny, call it what you will and believe what you will. After all only you know for sure, and in the end all that's required of you is to become the person you were meant to be, according to your beliefs.

Should we meet and experience instant rapport,

Could it be because we've met before?

A Life Well Lived

Copyright © Beverly Dewhirst 2015

Beverly Dewhirst has asserted her right under the copyright Designs and Patents Act 1988 to be identified as the author of this work.

This novel is a work of fiction. Names and characters are the product of the author's imagination and any resemblance to actual persons living or dead is entirely coincidental. This book is sold subject to the condition that it shall not, by way of trade or otherwise, be lent, resold, hired out or otherwise circulated without the author's prior consent in any form of binding or cover other than that in which it is published and without a similar condition, including this condition, being imposed on the subsequent purchaser.

First published in Great Britain 2015

ISBN9781508731825

Printed in Great Britain
by Amazon